SECOND CHANCES IN MONATANA

SECOND CHANCE ROMANCE

COWBOYS OF RIVER JUNCTION

LUCINDA RACE

MC TWO PRESS

Second Chances in Montana is a rewrite of Apple Blossoms in Montana. The story has been revised and expanded to a full-length novel and is now the first novel in the Cowboys of River Junction Series.

Editor Wendee Mullikin, Purple Pen Wordsmithing
Cover design by Jody Kaye
Manufactured in the United States of America
First Edition April 2024

Print Edition ISBN 978-1-954520-79-0
E-book ISBN 978-1-954520-78-3

AUTHORS NOTE

Hi and welcome to my world of romance. I hope you love my characters as much I do. So, turn the page and fall in love again.

If you'd like to stay in touch, please join my newsletter. I release it twice per month with tidbits, recipes, and an occasional special gift just for my readers, so sign up here: https://lucindarace.com/newsletter/, and there's a free book when you join!

Happy reading...

*Q*UICK NOTE: If you enjoy Second Chances in Montana, be sure to check out my offer for a FREE novella at the end. With that, happy reading

"*A*re you sure you're ready to take over River Bend Orchard? It's a big job for just one person." Her mom placed a hand over Renee's before she could scrawl her signature. With a balled-up tissue in her other hand, her mother's brow furrowed when she looked at Renee's dad. "Dave, I'm not sure about this anymore. We know how hard it is to run this business—the weather's fickle and financial margins can get razor thin. I think we should just sell out to that man, Lucas Gasperini, and give our girl her share now before we leave for Arizona."

Taking her mother's hand, her dad gave Renee a questioning look. As if silently asking whether she wanted to change her mind.

Renee shook her head.

"Sara, this is something Renee has been waiting for and we haven't foisted the orchard upon her. Besides, we're not moving to Siberia; we'll be available for advice." Her dad nodded, smiling. The corners of his eyes crinkled and deep dimples formed in his cheeks—just like they'd done every time he was proud of her. "And if you ever decide you do want to sell, we'll support that too."

Renee pressed a hand to her rumbly midsection, wishing she had filled it with breakfast before they left the house. She dipped her head, despite the enormity of carrying on the family legacy, her insides danced with excitement.

Willing herself to relax, she inhaled and exhaled several times. Her chest rose and fell as she reclaimed her inner balance like she had done so many times in yoga.

It had taken years to convince them it was time to pass the tractor keys on and let her control her destiny. The last thing she needed was for her parents to view this as a frivolous idea.

Her voice was clear and steady. "Dad, I appreciate your concern—and Mom, you too—I'm excited to put the city in the past and return to my roots. River Junction is where I belong. It's where I want to live. Please trust that I'm capable of handling the orchard. You've laid a strong foundation—not just with the business, but with me too."

Her mom patted her hand. She tipped her head to the side and looked deep into Renee's eyes. "Not a single second thought?"

"Not from me, but it sounds like you and Dad might not be ready to move to the desert." She hoped her tone came off light and breezy.

Her dad's health wasn't the best and the doc had said he needed to slow down. With his sky-high blood pressure and cholesterol and the stress of running the business, he was a heart attack waiting to happen. His best chance at a long life was to make a significant change.

"I understand this is difficult being that Dad has

2

worked the land since he was eighteen. Then you guys got married and became the second generation to run the orchard and you worked to expand it even more. Granddad always said you and Dad had the magic touch when it came to apples. Now it's my turn to see if I can carry on and make you proud of me."

Her mom placed a hand over her heart. Her voice cracked as she said, "Renee, we've always been proud and you don't need to take over the farm to prove that to us, if that's what you're doing."

Renee knew she had to convince them, even if Robert Adler, who had been the family lawyer for as long as she could remember, was charging them by the minute. "I never said anything because I didn't want to worry you, but I hated living in Chicago. All the noise, pollution, and rude people. Don't get me started on trying to find a crisp, juicy apple freshly picked—the kind where the juice runs down your chin when you take that first bite. It's like looking for ninety-degree temps in River Junction in December."

Her dad chuckled and her mom exhaled. A smile hovered in her eyes. Even if they thought it was a stretch about buying a fresh apple, they'd appreciate her attempt at humor. Her brow quirked in her parents' direction. She tapped the polished walnut table with the tip of the fancy black and gold trimmed pen and pulled the contract to her. "I'm ready to sign if you are."

Her mom leaned forward and tucked a lock of Renee's long hair behind her ear. She looked into her daughter's eyes as Renee glanced away as if her mother might see the secret which lingered there.

But the secret Renee held back was that she had lost her job due to downsizing and this was her best chance at enjoying a happy and normal life. Besides, the stress was causing her blood pressure to skyrocket and getting out of

3

the corporate rat race was just what her doctor had ordered.

Renee's mom cupped her chin. "If you ever change your mind, you can sell the orchard and your dad and I wouldn't be upset. All we've ever wanted for you was to live your best life."

She loved her parents, but she swore that sometimes they forgot she wasn't a kid in school. High school graduation was twenty years ago and since, she received a college degree and then worked in the city. In her off hours she had wondered if she would be happier in the small Montana town. "Since we agree that we all need to live our best lives, let's sign this paperwork and run over to the Filler Up Diner for a celebratory lunch. After that, we'll head home and get your Blazer packed so you'll be ready to hit the road after the sun comes up." With the pen poised over the signature line, she gave her parents a side-glance. "After all, you have a house closing to get to in three days."

She boldly scrawled her name across the legal document. When the last loop on the *L* was written, she handed the fancy pen to her father. "Your turn."

He didn't hesitate and her mom did the same before sliding the papers across the polished table in Mr. Adler's direction.

He glanced over the contract, nodding at each page that had been signed and initialed. "Dave, helping you and Sara complete this deal makes me think that I should retire sometime in the near future too. But before that happens, I'll need a good lawyer to walk through the door and want to take over my practice. I'd never leave the folks of River Junction without legal support."

Dave reached across the table and clasped his hand, vigorously pumping his arm. "Rob, once we get settled, why don't you come down for a visit and check out the area? See if it's someplace you'd want to live or if you'd rather enjoy your retirement in River Junction."

"Thanks, Dave. I'll take you up on your offer." He pushed his chair back, the wooden legs screeching across the oak flooring, and shook her mom's hand too. "Sara, always a pleasure."

Mr. Adler turned toward Renee then clasped her hand in his. He studied her from under thick salt-and-pepper eyebrows. In a deep fatherly voice, he said, "Congratulations, Renee. And remember, if you need anything, just let me know. Business or personal, I'm just a phone call away."

"Thank you, Mr. Adler. I appreciate that." She gave him a warm smile, knowing the offer was genuine. There were very few people in town or on the surrounding ranches who wouldn't lend a hand if needed.

That was something else she had missed living in Chicago. Heck, she couldn't even name the people who lived on the same floor at her condo much less ask them for help should she have needed any.

"Would you like to join us? I'll bet Maggie has a great lunch special," Renee asked.

Mr. Adler's eyes twinkled. "Thank you, but enjoy the time with your folks."

Her dad tapped the top of the conference table on his way out and called over his shoulder, "Rob, we expect to see you in Arizona soon."

He lifted a hand. "Just let me know when you're up for company and I'll pack my bags."

Stepping from the porch to the sidewalk, the cool air felt good on Renee's cheeks after sitting in the overly warm conference room. She zipped her down jacket to her chin and shivered, patting her pockets, disappointed to discover they were empty. Then she jammed her hands in the zippered openings. The frosty nip in the air signaled fall had settled in and winter wouldn't be far behind. They hurried across the street and strolled down the cement sidewalk in the direction of the diner. Her parents held hands like they were teenagers.

A stab shot through Renee's heart and almost took her breath away. At one time she had someone special in her life and they had promised they'd always be together. But what did high school kids know of love and the demands of the real world? Hank Shepard was a distant memory, and thankfully, he lived fifteen hundred miles away. Not that she had kept up with his life, but her mom had casually mentioned his whereabouts when she arrived two weeks ago.

"Here we are." Her dad pulled open the heavy glass door.

Her mom kissed his cheek before she walked in. "Thank you, dear."

The busy diner buzzed with conversation. Townsfolk were catching up over a good meal at the local hot spot. The aroma of French fries and fried chicken wafted across the room, setting Renee's taste buds into anticipatory overdrive.

Maggie's food was the best within a hundred-mile radius—well, except for fancy dinners at the River Run Inn and of course, the best nachos were at The Lucky Bucket.

Maggie grabbed menus from the counter and hurried over to greet them. Her eyes sparkled as she said, "Hey, Mitchell family. All done with Rob?"

"The River Bend Orchard officially has a new owner." Beaming, her dad didn't attempt to keep his voice low as he wrapped his arm around Renee's shoulders.

A smattering of applause rang out and it grew until everyone at the diner was on their feet, smiling and clapping.

Renee felt heat rush to her cheeks, which flamed easily

and would *not* be flattering with her auburn hair. *Not that there is anyone I need to impress.*

Henry Shepard ambled her way. He had the gait of a man who had been in a saddle most of his life. He clapped her dad on the shoulder and gave her mom a half hug before giving her a fatherly embrace. "Renee, it doesn't matter what happened between you and that thickheaded son of mine. If you ever need anything, we're just over yonder on the neighboring ranch and never more than a phone call away."

"Thank you, Henry." She wanted to proclaim that she wouldn't need anything from a Shepard, but it was foolish to hold any animosity against Henry or his wife Maeve; they had always been sweet to her.

"Come to dinner on Sunday. Maeve would love to see you and Sara before you take off."

Her dad shook his head. "We're leaving early tomorrow, but we'll be back during the holidays. Maybe we can get together then."

Henry grinned. "I'll hold you to that, but Renee,"—he turned his attention to her—"dinner's at six and I won't take no for an answer."

She hesitated and he said, "Maeve and I run out of things to talk about on occasion, so you'd be doing us a favor."

That was a bold-faced fib. It was easier to agree to have dinner—and he *had* said it was just the two of them. There was no chance she'd run into either of their sons. "I'd love to. I'll give Maeve a call to see what I can bring."

He laughed. "You can ask, but plan on just bringing yourself. My bride will love cooking for someone besides me—and don't say no to leftovers. She'll send you home with them anyway."

"Thank you for the invitation, Henry. You said six?"

"Come any time after five. That way we can catch up on

7

what's been happening in your life for the last few years." He shook her parents' hands and reminded them to stay in touch before returning to his table.

Her mom pointed to a vacant booth where Maggie had placed menus on the table. "I'm famished and we should eat. Who knew selling an orchard could stimulate an appetite?"

Renee looked over her shoulder to where Henry sat.

He caught her eye and gave her a wink, just like he did when she was a kid hanging out in the stables at Stone's Throw Ranch.

A twist of her heart was a good reminder she had grown up…even if she hadn't completely moved on.

"Mom?" She slid into the bench seat across from her parents. "Did Maggie mention the specials for today?"

Her mom handed her a small handwritten page which began with fried chicken and ended with beef stew.

Renee scanned the list and smiled as she lifted her eyes to look at her parents. "We're getting three slices of huckleberry pie since I know you won't be ordering that anyplace in Phoenix."

Maggie stopped at their table. Her smile was as wide as the Colorado River. "Did I hear you mention pie? Are we skipping lunch and diving right into dessert?"

"Not likely," Renee's dad said. "I'd like the pot roast dinner and then pie with ice cream."

Her mom handed Maggie the menu and said, "Make that two. I can't make pot roast like you."

The waitress and owner of the Filler Up stood a little straighter and her smile grew even wider at the compliments. "And for you, sugar?"

Renee and Maggie were just about the same age, but she had always called Renee some sort of pet name. "Since I'll be able to enjoy the many delights of your menu for years to come, why don't you surprise me—and I will be having the pie too. Oh and…" She looked at the counter where the drink area was set up. She grinned when she saw the pale-yellow liquid in a glass dispenser. "A glass of your famous lemonade."

She jotted down their order on a small pad of paper. "Comin' right up." With that, she glided to the next table, giving those folks the same personal attention she had given to Renee and her parents.

Renee sighed. "I hope my business is half as successful as Maggie's."

Her mom reached across the table and gave her a reassuring pat on her hand. "You've got drive and determination on your side as well as a wealth of knowledge about running the orchard. I have no doubt you'll be a smashing success."

Renee looked out the large plate-glass window over the small town that she called home. That nervous, jangling feeling she had in her stomach less than an hour ago had evaporated. She'd made the only decision for her—and the right one for River Bend Orchard, too. *Everything is going to work out; I can feel it in my bones.*

2

*R*enee arrived at Stone's Throw Ranch for Sunday dinner as the sky turned a dusky purple. She glanced at her watch, realizing she had some time to spare. Lingering in her car, memories of the last time she'd been at the ranch with Hank constricted her heart.

It was the night before they would leave for college. They had clung to each other in the haybarn with heartfelt kisses and a promise not to let anything change and drive them apart. In hindsight, it was naïve to think distance wouldn't change everything. The physical and emotional space between them had become a chasm never to be crossed. In those first couple of months, they had tried, but the demands of homework, part-time jobs, and new friends made it easier to just let their romance get pushed to the back burner.

Much like the Colorado River raging in spring, sluicing around bends and turns, forcing a change in the flow of water, that's what college had been like for her—constantly changing.

She shivered as the warmth dissipated from the car. *Time to walk the short distance to the main house.* Straightening her shoulders, she repeated over and over as the distance closed, *You can do this. You can do this.*

The sounds of cattle lowing reached her ears, offering reassurance that the ranch hadn't changed much. Except tonight Hank wouldn't swing open the door and pull her into his arms for a quick kiss with a promise of more to come later.

She tapped on the back door, holding a jug of apple cider, even though when she had chatted with Maeve on the phone she was told to just come hungry. But that didn't seem right, and it had been drilled into her since she was little to never show up at someone's home for a meal empty-handed. The cider was some of the best her family had pressed in years.

A woman's voice called out, "Come in, door's open."

Renee stepped into the warm, spacious kitchen. It was as if she had stepped back in time by twenty years.

Maeve Shepard was stirring a pot of gravy and she hadn't changed a bit, except there were a few strands of silver in her dark-brown hair. But the welcoming smile in her soft caramel-brown eyes said it all.

This was still Renee's second home. She then noticed her second favorite smell: the scent of yeast hanging heavy in the air. Her mouth watered. *Will there be Maeve's famous dinner rolls with supper?*

"Renee." The older woman swept her into a bear hug. "It's so good to see you. It's been far too long." She took a step back and gave Renee a quick look from her toes to her eyes. "You haven't changed a bit."

With a nervous laugh, Renee said, "Maeve, you might need to run into Bozeman and get your eyes checked. I've gained twenty pounds since the last time you saw me."

With a dismissive wave of her hand, she smiled. "You always were too skinny, and you look fantastic. Glad to see you didn't change your hair color. I'd kill to have that shade of auburn and those waves." Her smile remained while they talked.

Renee held out the jug of cider. "Truth be told, I've never had time to sit that long in a salon. Work at the agency was never-ending, and there wasn't much time for frivolous appointments." What she didn't say was most of the tough projects landed on her desk since her boss was notorious for dating the new hires. In Renee's opinion, they were hired based on looks and not talent.

Maeve took the jug and placed it on the counter. "Dinner will be ready soon. You didn't have to bring anything; we've got plenty." She gestured to the kitchen table that was set for three, complete with platters and bowls, and the aromas emanating from the oven made Renee's mouth water.

"There seems to be a lot of serving dishes over there."

She shrugged. "You know me, I love to cook. Besides, it's hard to get out of the habit of cooking for two growing boys. Henry and I eat for days off one dinner, but he doesn't complain. I've tried cooking for two but gave up when I discovered it made me sad looking at two pork chops, two potatoes, and a couple of spoonsful of gravy." Maeve squeezed Renee's arm. "And be prepared. You're taking leftovers home and I won't take no for an answer."

She stuffed her gloves in the pockets of her jacket and slipped it off, hanging it on the coatrack next to the back door. "But Maeve, you don't need to do that. I can cook."

She flashed Renee that side-eye look that she had seen countless times growing up. It wouldn't do any good to state the obvious because Maeve, like her own mom, thought they always knew best.

"Would you pop into the den and let Henry know you're here? It would be nice to visit before dinner is ready."

"Do you need help?"

Maeve pointed to the archway that led into the other room. "No. Just tell my husband to stop watching football and come to the kitchen. He knows I hate it when I'm finishing dinner and instead of visiting, he's watching grown men run up and down a field, deliberately pushing the others down." She shook her head. "I know my boys both played, but I never understood the appeal."

She plopped a kiss on Maeve's cheek. "It's an acquired taste and don't tell anyone, but I agree with you."

The older woman grinned. "And that's why you were always my favorite girl."

Renee strolled into the den, noticing little had changed in there. There were new his-and-hers recliner chairs and a wall-mounted flat screen dominating the opposite wall, but the rest was exactly the same. "Hi, Henry."

He pointed the remote at the screen and the exuberant announcer's voice faded to nothing. A smile warmed his eyes. "Renee, it's good to see you. Want to watch the game?"

"Sorry, no. I was sent to tell you dinner will be ready soon and to come into the kitchen so we can catch up."

He glanced at the television. "That's too bad. My wife has a knack for requesting my presence at the exact moment the game gets interesting." Pushing the footrest closed, he stood up. "Did your mom and dad get off okay?"

"They did, and they're busy unpacking. Dad said the weather is perfect."

They walked into the kitchen as Maeve tapped the keys on the laptop which sat on the counter. Without looking up, she said, "Hank's on video. He knows we're having supper soon, but he wants to say hello."

Rubbing his hands together and with a pep in his step, Henry hurried around to the other side of the counter and sat on stool. Renee guessed it was a normal Sunday evening occurrence.

"Hello, son. I'm sure your mom told you we're just getting ready to eat." He glanced at Renee. "And tonight, we have company." Waving to her, he beamed like he had a Christmas secret. "You'll never guess who."

She held up her hand and shook her head, wishing she could sink through the floor. The last thing she needed was to see Hank Shepard's handsome face. It had been eons since they had even spoken.

Henry held out his hand and wiggled his fingers in her direction. She was going to have to be polite, as much as it might kill her. She crossed the room and hovered over his right shoulder, but her eyes locked on Hank. Her heart constricted with that old familiar pain she had fought so hard to forget.

"Hiya, Hank."

His eyes widened and quickly returned to normal.

Catching him off guard gave her a tiny bit of satisfaction.

"Renee, I didn't know you were in town."

She wasn't about to confess that she had left Chicago and taken over the orchard. *Keep it casual, give away nothing.* "Yup, and your parents were nice enough to invite me for dinner."

"Well, good. I'm glad." He rubbed a hand across his chin and looked away from the screen. "You know, Dad, why don't I call back during the week? Go enjoy your company and dinner while it's hot."

Maeve said, "We're home all but Wednesday. Dad and I are going to have dinner at the Filler Up. Maggie's having barbeque night and you know I love good pulled pork and baked beans."

"I'll keep that in mind. Have a good night and talk soon." The screen faded to a picture of a horse.

Renee eased away from Henry. Her fingertips tingled and her belly fluttered. Sitting down was a great idea before she made a fool of herself by passing out. Grabbing the side of the table, she waited as her breathing slowly returned to normal.

Why hadn't she considered the possibility he might call his parents? Didn't most people call their loved ones on a Sunday before their week got busy? At least this was better than an in-person run-in. So now if they bumped into each other, maybe it would be less awkward. After all, River Junction was a small ranching community and he did come home to visit family from time to time—but tonight, she hadn't been ready to see the only man she had ever loved.

Henry pushed back from the counter. "Renee, sit in your old spot." He pointed to the chair she had sat in years before when she and Hank were a couple. *Good thing he doesn't seem to notice my mini freak-out.* Dang, this was comforting and odd at the same time.

Maeve hung her apron on a hook near the sink and sat in the chair that Henry had pulled out for her.

Renee sighed. Thankfully, some things never changed and sadly some had.

꽃

*H*ank closed his laptop as his shoulders sagged. He took several deep, shaky breaths as he collapsed into the leather chair. Seeing Renee Mitchell in his parents' kitchen after all these years had been a gut punch. Why hadn't his mom texted him to say they wouldn't be able to chat at their usual time? She didn't need to tell him who was coming for dinner, but dang, Renee looked fantastic. He remembered how a lock of her silky auburn hair felt as he twirled it around his index finger while they sat together on a hay bale. Stargazing had been one of their favorite pastimes and the show any time of the year never disappointed. Now he had questions galore. He should have asked how long she'd be in town. Maybe they could get together during the holidays for a coffee or even a beer at The Lucky Bucket. But did he want to travel down memory lane and rip open old wounds? He knew he'd broken her heart and the promise he had made that different colleges wouldn't matter. Besides, who finds their soul mate as little kids? That's the stuff of movies, not reality.

He pushed back from the desk and paced in front of the windows, oblivious to the stunning sunset dipping below the Dallas skyline. That brief glimpse of Renee was a razor-sharp reminder his life was empty. He never found another woman who challenged him, laughed with him, or loved him—not like Renee. Instead, he settled for his career. Life was good, money was plentiful, and the work was challenging at the law firm. And now he was a junior partner. A few good friends and work weren't enough to fill the moments late at night when he wished different choices had been made.

He walked into the kitchen and grabbed a long-neck bottle of beer from the refrigerator, tossing the cap into the garbage bin. Taking a long pull of the ice-cold brew, he closed his eyes, willing her beautiful face from his mind. *For now*. There was one thing about Renee Mitchell…she was the one woman he never truly got over and he had to accept the fact he never would.

3

The holiday season had come and gone and Renee had managed to avoid the Stone's Throw Ranch holiday party *and* Hank Shepard. Her parents had gone and casually mentioned he was there, but she didn't want to see him.

Dodging snowstorms, her parents made the return trip to Arizona with a promise to come back at some point in the summer.

Renee had spent the months of January and February planning the acreage for the east parcel. If all went according to plan, she'd plant ten acres with new stock once spring arrived. That was, of course, if Mother Nature cooperated and the ground was workable.

In the kitchen, the woodstove pumped out glorious heat. Renee leaned against the doorjamb while she studied the barns through the glass. A mug of coffee warmed her chilled hands. Plans for upgrading and expanding the industrial kitchen were almost ready—it would go in the barn with the cider press.

Thank goodness she had managed to press all the apples she needed to get a substantial stash of cider before the old press conked out. Once the days got a little warmer, she'd have Tony Hall come out and overhaul it so it would be up and running for next season.

When she finished her coffee, she rinsed the cup and sat wrapped in the silent cocoon of her home. Most days, the quiet didn't bother her, but that day it was getting on her last nerve.

Never one to be idle, it was time to saddle her old gelding, Darby, and take a ride along the orchard path visualizing what the orchard would look like when the new trees were heavy with fruit. As long as she went slow and avoided icy patches, they both would be fine. The last thing she'd want to do was hurt the horse all because she needed to escape the house and feel semi-useful.

As she stood contemplating what else she needed to get done—other than wishing the snow would melt—the house phone rang. Annoyed that another telemarketer would be on the other end, she grumbled, "Hello."

"Renee, it's Maeve." Her words came in short bursts. "Thank goodness you're home. I need help. Henry fell. Could you come over?"

She was already sliding her feet into the thick-soled winter boots beside the back door. "I'm on my way."

Wrenching the keys to the pickup truck off the hook, she grabbed her coat and raced across the drive to the barn. Without knowing how badly Henry was hurt, she wasn't sure what to expect. She tugged on the sliding barn door but it was frozen in the track. Cursing at it, she pushed with all her strength, every way she could, to loosen it. Finally, it broke free. She leaped into the driver's seat, backed the truck out, and jogged back to the barn to slid the door closed—so Darby and a couple of barn cats who lived in a connected part of the barn would stay warm. As she hit every rut in the gravel driveway, she wished there had been time to make sure there was plenty of food and water for the animals. There was no telling how long she'd be gone.

Her hands gripped the wheel, taking care to avoid the swale on the right side. If she hit just one patch of ice, she'd be in the ditch and of no help to the Shepards. The shortcut between the orchard and the ranch was the quickest route and she had used it last Sunday when she had gone for her monthly dinner with them. It would have been smoother to take the highway, but that would add another fifteen minutes to her trip. Glancing at her watch, she wondered if she should call Hank but refocused on the dirt lane. Before calling, she would check with Maeve. No sense in getting him all riled up if this was nothing.

Taking the turn onto the long gravel road without hitting the brakes, Renee's tires spun as she fishtailed, kicking up stones. She skidded to a stop and threw the truck into park before jumping out. Leaving the truck door ajar and at a dead run, Renee rushed into the house, shouting, "Maeve. Henry."

Maeve's muffled response reached her. "In the den."

She hurried around the corner. Henry was lying on his back, his face ashen, pain etched around his thinned lips.

Dropping to her knees, she took his clammy hand in hers and glanced at Maeve. "What happened?"

She nodded in the direction of what might have been a stack of books, now scattered over the floor. "He tripped." She clung to his other hand. "I've been reminding him to put his reading material on the table but he liked it within easy reach. Now look. He says he can't get up, and he can't move his hip or leg. I called for an ambulance."

He growled, "But my back is fine."

At least he wasn't unconscious. "Henry, does it hurt anywhere else and do you want to try and get to a sitting position?"

He glanced Renee's way. "No, it doesn't hurt any place

19

other than my leg. It's a searing pain like I've never felt in my life."

That said a lot. Henry had been raised on a ranch and he was always injured with one thing or another—an occupational hazard around cattle and horses.

"You could have broken a hip so you need to stay quiet until help arrives."

He answered with an almost imperceptible nod. "Good idea."

The wail of a siren reached them, and Renee got to her feet. "I'll bring them inside."

Maeve fought back tears—it was as if his pain was her pain.

Renee turned away from them and jogged to the kitchen door. The ambulance had backed in and two of her old friends from high school, Nina and Josie, were gathering supplies and a gurney from the back.

Josie pushed the gurney toward Renee. "What happened?"

Nina was right behind her, carrying two oversized boxes that looked more like they held fishing tackle.

"Henry tripped over some books and is complaining of hip and leg pain and he can't sit up. I'm not an expert but he might have broken a hip." She pushed the door wide to make room for the gurney. "They're in the den just down the hall on the left."

The ladies went ahead of her and she lingered in the doorway as they began asking Henry questions about his pain level, what day and year it was, and if he knew where he was.

His eyes were closed but his voice was steady and sure with all his answers.

Renee exhaled a breath she had been holding. It was clear he had his wits about him.

After a brief examination, Nina said, "Henry, it's probable you broke your hip. But I want you to keep nice and still. We'll lift you onto the gurney and get you to the clinic. If it's a hip, you get an express ride to Bozeman for a bit of baling twine and super glue that will fix you right as rain on the range."

Renee suppressed a smile. Nina knew exactly how to talk to Henry to keep him calm.

He opened one eye. "You two can't lift me. I've packed on a few pounds in recent years. Maybe Renee could get a couple of the hands to help?"

"That's not necessary. We've got ways of moving you and with the least amount of pain possible."

He gave her a serious look. "I take it this might hurt a bit?"

She nodded as she double-checked his blood pressure. "It will and I can't give you anything for the pain. The doc needs to assess you first."

"I'm tough."

Maeve smiled and placed her hand over his. "You are and I'll be right beside you the entire time."

Josie adjusted the gurney so it was perpendicular to her patient. "Maeve, I'm sorry. You can't ride in the back of the ambulance."

Renee took a step forward. "It's okay, I'll drive her."

Henry closed his eyes. "Renee, find Joe Costello. He should be around the barns, maybe in the office, and let him know that I'm going to the clinic, but I'll be back as soon as I can. He needs to make sure everything runs smoothly around here." His voice was noticeably weaker.

She glanced at Maeve who nodded. "Check the office first and by the time you get back to the house, we can head into town."

"Sure thing. I'll be back as fast as I can." Withdrawing her truck keys from the jacket pocket, she knew it would be quicker to drive down in case she had to go looking for him. Even though the ranch wasn't as busy in winter at this time of day, Joe could be almost anywhere— working in the office, fixing a downed fence, or even looking for a steer who decided to roam.

Parking the truck in front of the door that had a small wooden sign announcing OFFICE, she didn't bother to turn off the truck. Best to keep it running so it would stay warm.

She pushed open the door, calling, "Joe?"

"Renee, that you? I'm right here, no need to shout." He pushed the chair back from the desk and stood. "Somethin' I can do for you? I haven't seen you around here in a long time." The ranch foreman was short in stature but made up for it in muscle—which was evident by the way the heavy sweatshirt strained over his biceps.

"Henry fell and is being taken by ambulance to the clinic. Josie and Nina suspect a broken hip and I'm going out on a limb to say he'll be transferred to Bozeman tonight. He wanted me to ask if you'd look after things until he gets back."

He pushed back his dark-brown Stetson, his brows knitted together, and he stuck his hands in his jeans pockets. "Of course. Anything he needs. Let him know I'm sending good thoughts. And Maeve too."

"Thanks. If you give me your cell number, I can let you know what's going on."

He scrawled the digits on a scrap of paper and handed it to her. "I'd appreciate that. Are you gonna call Hank and Ford?"

"Not yet, unless of course Maeve wants me to. Right now, we're going to follow the ambulance and wait to speak to the doctor. That's as far as I've gotten."

He gave a brief nod. "Alright. Thanks for helping Maeve out. She must be a wreck and I wouldn't want her driving all keyed up."

With a hand on the doorknob, Renee said, "It's what

they'd do for me if I needed help." She closed the door behind her and climbed into the truck. She pulled away from the office and drove to the house. There wasn't a thing she could do other than support a woman who must be worried sick about her husband.

*A*fter reaching the medical clinic, Renee waited in the emergency room for what seemed like an eternity.

Maeve finally appeared through the heavy metal door. Her shoulders slumped and her face had seemed to age a decade in a few hours. She carried the weight of the world on her shoulders.

Renee leaped up and wrapped the older woman in a hug. "How's Henry?"

"Resting. It's a broken hip. They're waiting on a transfer to Bozeman. He needs surgery, which will most likely be tomorrow. Tonight, they'll just get him settled and keep him comfortable. It will be a few hours before he leaves here. Apparently, there's a good orthopedic doctor who has a lot of experience working on tough rancher types like my husband. Doc Thorn said she's the best chance for him to ride again with as little discomfort as possible."

Renee steered her to a chair. "What about calling Hank and Ford? They should know what's going on."

"I know but Hank will rush up from Dallas and Ford will want to come but he's got my grandson Toby to look after." She frowned. "Not like the boy's mother would help. She's always flitting off somewhere." Her eyes widened and her mouth formed a large O. "I'm sorry, I shouldn't be airing Ford's dirty laundry."

Renee patted her hand. "I won't repeat a word. You've got a lot on your mind right now. What do you say I run you home and you can change clothes and we can meet Henry in Bozeman?"

"That sounds like a good plan, but I wouldn't want to trouble you."

"I offered so you have to take me up on it."

Tears formed in Maeve's eyes and she blinked them away. With a catch in her voice, she said, "You're a good person, Renee. And you're right. I must call the boys."

It was endearing that she still called her adult sons *boys*, something neither of them had been for over two decades.

"I'll give you some privacy." She got up and Maeve held tight to her hand.

"Please stay in case they have questions and I get flustered." She pulled a tissue from the sleeve of her sweater and dabbed her damp eyes. "This is all just so much."

Sinking back to the chair, Renee said, "I'll be right here if you need me."

Maeve dug into her bag and pulled out her wallet, a comb, a package of tissues, and a roll of Life Savers before she withdrew her cell. Handing the phone to Renee, she dumped the rest back in her bag. She took a deep breath. "Time to tell the boys." She tapped a couple of buttons and waited. "Hello, Ford, it's Mom. There's nothing to get excited about but your dad broke his hip and he's getting transferred to Bozeman. He'll have surgery tomorrow. You don't need to come but I wanted you to know. I'll give you a call later. Love you, honey." She hadn't given him the opportunity to ask questions and now that she had paused, her face scrunched up. "I told you everything I know at this point. Once Dad is settled in his hospital room, I'll call you." She paused again. "Yes, I promise. Goodbye, son."

Maeve exhaled a breath that seemed to come from her toes. "One down, one to go." She tapped a few keys.

Renee nodded, figuring Hank would likely pick up on

the first ring since he'd probably still be in his office at this time of day. She could hear him say, "Hey, Mom."

She gave Renee a weak smile and held up one finger. He had answered after just one ring.

"Honey, Dad's broken a hip and we're headed to Bozeman General for surgery. I thought you'd want to know."

Renee heard him shout, "What? Wait, give me the details."

Dr. Thorn came into the waiting room and motioned for Maeve to join her. Thrusting the phone at Renee, she said, "Can you fill him in? The doctor needs to speak with me."

Renee took the phone as a lead weight dropped into her stomach. She sucked in a ragged breath, reminding herself this was for Maeve and she could push her residual feelings aside. "Hank, it's Renee Mitchell."

---

4

*H*ank paced the length of his office as he thought of his dad going into surgery. "Tell me everything you know." It didn't matter that his words came out like a command or that he was treating Renee like a hostile witness on the stand in court. This was his father and he needed every detail. He clenched and unclenched his fist. *I will not be caught off guard when I walk into the hospital, that's not happening.* He could hear her take a slow, deep breath. Was his dad that bad or was talking to him so difficult? Who was he kidding? Just hearing her say his name was a gut punch. How many years did it take to purge a woman from your soul?

"First, both of your parents are fine." Renee's soothing voice was a balm to his shattered nerves. "Henry is in good hands and he'll be better once he has the surgery, but it will be a long recovery. Maeve is obviously distraught, but I've been with her since your dad fell. We're going to go back to the ranch and get your mom a change of clothes and some reading material before I drive her to Bozeman."

The knot in his gut lessened as she talked. "Any idea when the surgery is scheduled? Will it be tonight?" He glanced at his watch. There was no way he was getting a flight this late in the day.

"Tomorrow, late morning from what your mom said. He won't arrive at Bozeman General for several hours, between waiting for a transport ambulance and the actual drive. It all moves like molasses in winter."

"So, they don't have to take him by helicopter?"

"No, the hip is attached and he's not hemorrhaging from any orifice."

He heard the smile in her voice and knew his question had been over the top, but he was helpless to do anything from Dallas. It would take an hour or so to get a plan together. "What about Ford? Has she called him too?"

"She did but she kept it brief. I'm sure he'll call back later or maybe she'll call him, I'm not sure. Maeve doesn't expect him to fly out here; he has responsibilities in Tennessee."

Renee had no idea how loaded that statement was. He was positive Ford hadn't filled his parents in on the latest chapter in the saga of the so-called marriage featuring Ford and Sharon. When Ford was ready, he'd tell them. Sharon had walked out and cut all ties—not just with her husband, but her son too.

"Hank?"

"Sorry, lost my train of thought." He sank to a cushioned chair in the small sitting area and stretched his legs in front of him. "I'm going to catch the first available flight out and I'll go straight to the hospital. More than likely, I won't get there until midday tomorrow."

"Don't worry. I'll stay with your mom until you arrive."

He nodded and leaned forward, his forearms resting on his thighs. "Do you think you can convince Mom to sleep at home tonight and drive to Bozeman in the morning?"

She snorted a laugh. "Have you bumped your head recently? This is Maeve Shepard we're talking about. That woman could move a bull on a mountain if she needed to get to Henry."

He chuckled. That was an accurate description of his mom. He figured she needed to be tough after being a rancher's wife for over forty years. "I'm going to try and convince her."

"Good luck with that, but I plan on driving her to the hospital so please don't worry about her making the trip alone."

He swallowed the lump in his throat. "Thanks, Renee. You being with them makes this bearable. I don't know how I can repay you. Maybe I could buy you dinner the next time I'm in town."

The line was silent for several long moments. "I don't think that's a good idea. Your thanks is enough. Oh wait, hold on a sec."

He could hear people talking but not what they were saying.

"Hank, your mom is done talking to the doc so I'm going to pass the phone back to her."

There was a rustling sound.

"Hello, Hank, are you still there?" His mom sounded calmer so he hoped that meant good news.

"I'm here, Mom. What's the update?"

"Dr. Thorn said the surgery will be scheduled for tomorrow. We won't know the exact time until the orthopedic doctor sees him tonight. As soon as I know more, I'll call and maybe you can fill in Ford too?"

"Are you going to stay home tonight and drive to Bozeman in the morning?"

"No, I'm not leaving your father alone."

The unmistakable steel in her voice made him smile despite the circumstances.

"Renee said she'd drive me and I'll take a few things with me to freshen up in the morning."

"But Mom—"

"Hank. I will not change my mind. This is not open for discussion. Now I need to get back to the ranch. I want to be at the hospital when your dad is brought in. I promise to call tonight. I love you, son, and please try not to worry. Your dad is in good hands and for that matter, so am I. Renee has been such a doll to stay with me."

"She mentioned she's going to take you back to the house."

Mom's voice dropped. "Since she is going to drive me to the hospital, will you call Joe Costello and ask him to take care of her animals? I don't want Renee to worry about anything at her place while she's helping us."

Even with the stressful situation looming, Mom was still thinking of others. "Consider it done and please tell Renee not only will Joe take care of the animals, but he'll check on things until she's back from Bozeman."

"Thank you, son. I need to see your father before I leave. Love you, honey, and try not to fret. I'll call you tonight."

"Don't worry about the time. Call whenever you need to talk." He didn't bother to tell her he would see her the next day. Let that be a little surprise. Mom hated flying and worried incessantly when he was on a plane. It was easier for both of them if he just showed up. "Love you, Mom, and tell Dad to listen to the medical professionals for a change."

"I'll try but you know your father." She let that statement trail off before saying, "I'll call you later."

He didn't move from the chair for several minutes, replaying the conversation in his head. He knew how upset she was since she had said four times that she'd call him tonight. At least she wasn't alone. Which prodded him to contact Joe first, and then he'd check on flights, check in with his boss, and pack. He'd work from Montana for the foreseeable future. Once Dad was able to go home, his parents would need help, and if nothing else, he could slip into his Levi's and cowboy boots and run the ranch.

*T*he next morning Hank strode through the Dallas Fort Worth airport terminal, silently clicking off the way the morning would flow. He had booked a nonstop flight scheduled to depart at eight twenty arriving at ten a.m. Once on the ground, he had an SUV rented and should be at the hospital by eleven. Dad's surgery was scheduled for one o'clock so there would be plenty of time to visit with him. Once Dad went down for the operation, lunch with his mom and Renee would round out the morning.

His heart ached at the thought of seeing Renee. In all these years, he had only seen her once—on the Facetime call a few months ago—and the years hadn't dimmed her beauty. He shook his head. *Stop sounding like a hokey love poem.* This was his former almost fiancée, and they had both moved on. Well, he was still trying.

Once through DFW security and at the gate, he used his suitcase for a table and spread out the sausage and egg bagel he bought at the fast-food place. His cell rang before he got the top off his coffee. Ford's face popped up on the screen.

"Hey, bro, thanks for calling me back. Have you talked with Mom this morning?" Ford's voice was laced with annoyance. But the dark circles under his eyes told a different story.

Instantly, Hank's hackles went up, but then he exhaled. His brother was under a lot of pressure as a single parent, navigating uncharted territory. He needed a break even if it was just this one conversation. "I talked to her but I had to get through airport security and to my gate. And thanks for asking, but yeah, I'm finally sitting down."

"Sorry, Hank. I'm on edge and you're the first adult I've

talked to this morning. Sharon hasn't called Toby once since she left and the kid's a mess. He didn't even want to go to school. I talked with his teacher and she said Toby thinks I'll abandon him too."

"That stinks, man. What can I do to help?"

He rubbed a hand over his face which did nothing to erase the haunted look in his eyes. "Nothing. I just needed to vent."

"I get it. We're both on edge for different and the same reasons." Hank picked up his coffee and blew on it before taking a sip. "I'm not sure how you're feeling but I've got a good case of the guilts."

"About the folks? Yeah, me too. So what did Mom say? Is Dad doing okay?"

"She stayed with him last night and the staff set up some kind of recliner chair for her in his room. I guess he had a decent night but he's grumpy this morning since he can't have coffee or breakfast."

Ford chuckled. "I pity those nurses. More painkillers are needed—that's if they work on grumpiness too."

"Understatement of the day." He looked around the terminal. A small family caught his attention, a husband, wife, and an adorable little girl with long red hair, hugging a teddy bear close to her chest. He was a bad judge of age, but she was smaller than Toby.

"What time is the surgery again? I know you told me but my head's like a sieve."

Hank said, "One o'clock. I should be at the hospital by eleven and I'll give you a call after I see them." The family moved in the direction of another gate. "Hey, do you think you can bring Toby to the ranch this summer? Spend some time with the folks?"

"I don't know with work and all. It's gonna be tough. I keep hoping Sharon will change her mind and want to see him. He keeps asking for her."

"Being with his grandparents might help." Hank knew it would also be good for their parents since Dad might not be able to ride for a long while. "Toby might be the best medicine to help Dad's recovery."

"I'll think about it."

"Ford, I know this sucks. But give it some thought and if money for tickets is tight I can—"

"You don't need to pay our airfare. If I want to take my son home, I can afford it."

There was no mistaking the prickly tone in Ford's voice. But it was good to hear he considered the ranch his home. "Just an offer, bro." He glanced at the clock above the door to the jet bridge. "I need to eat so I'm ready to board. I'll catch ya on the flip side."

"Alright, safe travels."

They said goodbye and Hank tossed his cell on top of his laptop bag. He'd lost his appetite when he thought of Toby and couldn't imagine what it would feel like to have someone important—like a mother—walk out on you. All the more reason to convince Ford to bring the boy to River Junction for a couple of weeks—possibly even the entire summer. Maybe Hank could even swing being around too. It would be fun hanging with Toby.

With that idea percolating, suddenly he was starving and devoured his bagel sandwich in no time. Gate activity continued to increase and soon people were standing around, anxious for boarding to begin.

Hank wondered if he'd bump into Renee at the hospital and how he would feel when they came face-to-face.

A voice crackled over the speaker and Hank strained to hear what was said. "Flight 1279 is now boarding with nonstop service to Bozeman, Montana. First-class passengers are welcome to board at this time."

Hank gathered his things and made his way toward the jet bridge door. Two hours from now, he'd be driving to the hospital. It didn't matter how he was feeling; he was a master at hiding what went on underneath his lawyer façade.

Renee would never know.

He scanned the boarding pass' QR code from his phone. The terminal beeped.

The gate attendant said, "Enjoy your trip, sir."

Hank thanked him. *Once Dad is on his way to a full recovery, I'll make the return trip to Dallas and everything will fall back into my neat and orderly, if solitary, life.*

He paused mid-step.

Did Renee have someone in her life and could he be living at the orchard with her? That was the one question he had shied away from in all conversations with his mom.

5

*R*enee sat outside Henry's hospital room, sipping lousy coffee from the hospital cafeteria—but at least it gave her a much-needed jolt of caffeine. She wanted to give the Shepards some privacy before the nurses came to take Henry down for surgery.

The last eighteen hours had seemed like forty-eight. Navigating the drive to Bozeman through the snowstorm wasn't fun. They had crept along at half the speed limit to get them there safely, but the exhaustion had seeped into her bones. Pretending to sleep on a hard vinyl-cushioned chair just in case Maeve needed something was the right thing to do. There was no way she would abandon Maeve before Hank arrived.

If she were being truthful, part of her wanted to bolt before he strode in. Even now, thinking of his broad shoulders and caramel-brown eyes that always held a hint of mischief caused her stomach to flip.

She stretched her neck from side to side, trying to work out the kinks, and walked to the large expanse of glass that overlooked the parking lot. From the second-story window, she saw her truck covered in a thick coating of snow. It had continued to snow another eight inches after they arrived. She placed her hand on the cold window. "March in Montana," she said softly.

The blue sky and bright sun were promising that spring would eventually produce warmer days, sans snowstorms, but you never knew in this part of the country. From her vantage point, at least the roads looked clear. A late model black Suburban caught her attention as it slid into the first open parking space near her truck. Her breath hitched in her chest.

She would recognize that man anywhere.

Hank.

He got out from behind the wheel, stretched his arms over his head, opened the back door, and pulled on a coat. Unable to look away, she watched him jog out of sight. It would only be a few moments before they would come face-to-face.

As much as she wanted to hide in the waiting room, she stood her ground. Better to face him and get it over with. There was no way she was going to hang around and try to keep up a façade of indifference when they had never cleared the air after their dispassionate breakup.

Renee strode to the bank of elevators. Her best defense was making the first move—well, at least in this situation. She ran a hand over her tangled head of hair, wishing she didn't look like she'd slept in a chair all night, even if that were exactly what she had done.

The doors slid open and his gaze ran from the tip of her boots to her eyes—the jolt of shock registering on his face.

A small glimmer of satisfaction wrapped around her heart. She knew that look.

The doors started to close when he thrust his hand out and stopped them. They silently slid open and he took a step closer to her. Dang, he looked good with his long jean-clad legs, shined black cowboy boots, and gray cable-knit sweater that looked touchably soft as it hugged his broad shoulders and skimmed his torso. He was as trim as he had been the summer before they left for college.

"Hank. It's good to see you." The fib slipped over her lips like water over an algae-covered rock in the Colorado River.

"Renee." He lightly kissed her cheek.

She knew it was a reflex, a gesture left over from before.

"Thanks for staying with my parents last night. I understand there was a storm; the drive in must have been rough."

Her insides twisted. "Not a big deal. Driving in snow is second nature to me, growing up here and then living in Chicago. Big on snow." *Why the heck am I rambling on about snow?*

She pointed down the hall. "Maeve is in with Henry." Taking a step in the direction she had pointed, he followed her.

Creased lines were etched between his eyes. "Was there any change overnight?"

"No. He rested and your mom pretended to sleep in the chair next to his bed, but if she'd gotten ten minutes of rest, I'd say that was a lot."

He glanced at her. "And you?"

The sincerity in his voice made a tiny chink in the armor she had carefully constructed to protect herself from Hank Shepard.

She tucked a stray wave behind her ear and looked away from him. "I hung out in the waiting room, just in case." They stopped at an open door. "This is your dad's room. I'll say goodbye and take off. I have animals to take care of and plowing to get done."

He held up a hand to stop her from walking away. "Mom had me call Joe last night. Everything should be in good shape at the orchard."

36

She frowned. "I thought he fed my animals, but there's still plowing to take care of."

"No. I got a text from Joe this morning with an update on your place and the ranch. He's cleared your roads and your animals have been fed."

A murmur of voices drifted into the hallway.

Hank said, "Are you coming?"

"Just for a minute." Renee walked in the room ahead of him and Henry's face brightened when he noticed Hank. She looked from father to son and was glad he had more family support now.

She stood at the foot of the bed, being careful not to bump it. "Henry, Maeve, I'm going to head back to River Junction. Is there anything I can do for you there?"

Maeve clasped Henry's hand and stretched out her free one to Renee. "Stay until after Henry is out of surgery. The doctor said it would take about two hours."

Squeezing Maeve's hand, she said, "I need to get back. I'm expecting a couple of phone calls and would hate to reschedule them. You know the life of a small business owner; our work waits for no one."

Henry gave her a painkiller-filled smile. "You're a good girl, Renee, and as soon as I get home, you need to come for dinner."

She laughed. "Henry, that's very sweet but not necessary. I was happy to help. Besides, now that Hank's here, I'm sure he can eat enough dinner so you won't need to eat days of leftovers. But if you need anything, I'm just a phone call away."

Henry nodded. "There is one thing you can do. Swing by the ranch and let Joe know that Hank's here so if anything comes up, he should call Junior. I don't want him bothering Maeve with ranch business." He smiled at his wife. "I know you pretended to sleep in that chair, but you need to rest too."

37

"Consider it done." Renee walked around the side of the bed where Maeve sat and kissed her cheek, then leaned over the bed and kissed Henry's cheek too. "Now, you make sure you do exactly what the nurses tell you for a speedy recovery."

He gave her a wink. "I'll do my best. I'm already missing the ranch and can't wait to get on my horse, check on the cattle, and ride the fence line."

Maeve kissed the back of his hand. "Dear, that's going to be a while yet. The doctor has already said it'll be six to eight weeks, more if you don't behave."

Renee skirted around the end of the bed, careful to avoid brushing up against Hank. "Don't rush it and let your body heal."

Maeve said, "Please text me when you get home. I know you spent a sleepless night in that awful chair."

She couldn't help the smile that filled her face. That was such a mom thing to say. "Sure, but please, don't worry about me. You've got enough on your mind."

Hank trailed behind her as they walked out of the hospital room. He touched her arm. "Thanks again for all you've done." He withdrew his wallet and held out a crisp one-hundred-dollar bill.

She took a step back. "What's that for?"

He pressed it into her hand. "Gas, as a small thank you."

A flicker of annoyance flared in her and she shoved it back at him. "Hank Shepard, have you lost your freaking mind? In these parts, neighbors help each other—or did you forget that? I would never take a dime for helping your parents. They needed me and they would have done the same if the roles were reversed."

He pressed it into her hand and closed his other on top of it. "Please."

Her mouth fell open, shocked at the insult. "Hang on to

your money. You can tip your housekeeper when you get back to Dallas." She turned on her heel, the sound of each boot connecting with the tile floor echoing in the quiet hallway.

Hank hurried after her, his long strides making short work of the physical distance between them. "Renee, wait. I didn't mean to offend you. It's just that…" The words died on his lips as he met her eyes. "Oh damn, I really stepped in it. I know that brown-eyed, hard-as-granite glare."

She nodded in the direction of Henry's room. "You should spend time with your father before they take him for surgery. Take care of yourself, Hank, and see you in another twenty years."

She jabbed the elevator door CLOSE button and felt somewhat satisfied as they came together just as Hank opened his mouth to speak. Finally, she had the last word. Her shoulders slumped. *But why doesn't that make me feel better?*

*A*s Renee got closer to River Junction, her stomach grumbled, reminding her dinner had been a bag of chips and breakfast was lousy coffee. The Filler Up Diner was five minutes away and she'd treat herself to a late lunch.

The clock on the dash read two fifteen. Maybe at this hour Maggie would have time for a quick chat. Rekindled friendships were what she needed now, before things got busy with planting. The quiet and isolation of the long winter months had caught her off guard. Growing up, she'd been busy with school activities and friends had come home from college with her.

Cruising down the open road, the radio belting out a Beatles tune, she grinned as a half-forgotten memory bubbled to the surface. Ginny Rhodes, her best friend in college, came to town every year for spring break instead of going to Florida or some other beach destination. She had wanted to spend the week ogling cowboys and promptly fallen in love with the raucous nightlife of The Lucky Bucket on Saturday and the hearty Sunday breakfast the next morning, but she couldn't understand why the cowboys hid during the week.

She flicked on her blinker and exited the highway for the two-lane road that would take her to downtown River Junction. Her cell rang and she grinned as she tapped the speakerphone button. "Hey, Ginny. I was just thinking about you."

Laughter filled the car. "Ree, I hope it wasn't about the time I decided to try hiking and toppled backward down the front steps of the apartment complex *after* I hoisted my backpack up."

"Nope, it was the first time you came to Montana with me. Remember you were hoping to fall in love with a real cowboy and all you got was one night being twirled around the dance floor at the local watering hole?"

"That was a blast. Which in a roundabout way brings me to why I'm calling. I was wondering, if you wouldn't mind, if I came out for a week or three."

Hearing the hesitation in her voice, Renee was quick to say, "You know the door's always open, but what's going on? I figured you and Aron were planning a wedding, date TBD."

There was a pregnant pause.

"Ginny, did I lose you?"

A soft sob reached Renee's ears. "No. We broke up and I could use a change of pace. I can finish my new cookbook anywhere as long as you don't mind lending me your kitchen for some final testing and be my official taster. Besides, he is going to buy me out of the condo, so effectively I'm homeless."

Giving a low whistle, Renee said, "Of course, you can come anytime. I'll get the guest room freshened up. Just tell me when you're arriving, and I'll pick you up at the airport."

"No need. I'm driving."

"From Chicago? That's like twenty hours in good weather and you have no idea how fickle it can be out here in the spring." Renee looked at the three-foot-high snowbanks on either side of the road.

Ginny huffed out a groan. "Alright, I'm going to tell you the entire plan. I bought an SUV and I'm packing the parts of my life I want to keep in it. I'm leaving Chicago for good. Once I turn my book into the publisher, I'll move around and figure out where I want to settle down. I'm tired of the city and need a change of pace. If I can stay with you for a bit, then I'll find a rental in that charming town of yours. I know you're thinking I'm nuts for leaving the place I've called home for almost fifteen years, but I thought you'd understand since you just did the same thing."

Renee wasn't going to point out she lost her job and this had been her home. That was a moot point and there had to be something more behind this breakup.

"Ree." A choked sob was followed by, "The jerk cheated on me and they're going to have a baby."

Hearing the heartache in her voice, Renee knew she'd welcome Ginny with open arms. "Make sure you buy long underwear before you hit the road. It gets pretty cold out here and it's a different kind of cold than Chicago."

"Renee, thank you." Her voice caught like she was full-on crying. "You have no idea what this means to me."

Gripping the wheel tighter, she responded, "Yeah, I think I do. A fresh start will make a difference in moving forward. I'm sorry for what happened but I'm proud that you're taking the leap. I'll give you a call later and we can talk about the route you're taking and what the best towns for you to stop in are."

"I knew calling you was the best idea. Talk to you later."

They said their goodbyes and Renee focused on the road in front of her. At least for the next couple of weeks, Ginny would keep her mind off Hank Shepard, and after that, he'd be back in Dallas.

6

*H*ank watched the elevator door silently close in front of his eyes with Renee on the other side. The last thing he saw was her cold, unflinching glare.

How could he have been so stupid to offer her money for helping his parents? The burden of blame for insulting her rested at his feet. The last thing he wanted was to feel like he owed her a return favor. But folks around River Junction were genuine; even a person he had hurt wouldn't hold that against his family.

With a slow, plodding walk, he made his way back to his dad's room. He could beat himself up later for all the things he had done wrong in regard to Renee—and not only including today.

Mom's eyes lit up as he entered the room, and then her brow arched. "Where's Renee?"

"Headed back to her place, but first she'll stop at the ranch and give Joe an update." He slumped into a plastic chair next to his dad's bed.

His parents exchanged a familiar look that usually meant he was about to get a talking to.

"Go ahead. I can take it."

As his dad tried to reposition himself on the bed, beads of sweat popped out on his forehead. Out of breath, he asked, "Son, did you and Renee argue?"

"Not really, but I managed to upset her when I offered her money." He stared at the floor to avoid his mother's *you did what?* glare.

She pursed her lips. "Why on earth would you do that?"

"I'm a bumbling idiot when it comes to her." He leaned forward, his arms resting on his thighs, and dropped his head. He couldn't feel much lower than he did right now. "Ever since I broke her heart after that first semester in college, I can't seem to make things good between us."

"Do you want to?" his dad asked.

Hank looked at him with a nod. "Yes, if I could change the present, I would definitely make up for the past."

"Sounds like you're looking for a second chance with the only woman you ever loved." His mom folded her arms across her chest and tipped her chin up. "What are you going to do about it?"

"Right now, nothing. I'm here to help you get Dad back on his feet, and then I'm going back to Dallas. I have a thriving law practice and that's good enough."

His dad snorted. "Keep telling yourself that, Hank. But a job won't give you the future you really want. Mark my words. You never met a woman who could hold a candle to Renee and you stopped trying, that's the real issue."

A nurse bustled into the room, pausing to hit the hand sanitizer pump on the wall. The glowing smile on her face spoke of a *rainbows and sunshine* kind of person. "Hello, Mr. Shepard, I'm Janey. I'm going to check your vitals and get you ready for the transport team. Good news. The doctor is on schedule so you'll have your new hip before you know it."

"The sooner the better," his dad mumbled.

"I just need to ask you a couple of boring questions."

The nurse ran through name, date of birth, day of the week and year before she gave Hank a direct look with one brow arched.

He raised his hand. "I'm Hank, the son from Dallas." He moved away from the bed in case he was in the way. "How long will the surgery take?"

Janey clipped a small meter on his dad's index finger and picked up his wrist, checking his pulse rate. "The doctor didn't tell you? Not long, just a couple of hours. You and your mother should get out of the hospital and grab a bite of lunch. There's a nice restaurant across the street."

"I'm not leaving him." His mother clutched his dad's hand.

"We have your cell number, Mrs. Shepard. Should we need to get in touch with you, I promise to call, but you've been by your husband's side since last night and a change of scenery would perk you up."

Henry said, "Maeve, go with Hank and get a hot meal. You'll have plenty of time to hover over me when I'm back in my room."

She chewed her bottom lip and looked from her husband to her son. "I don't know," she began. "What if…?"

Hank hated the conflict in her eyes. "I'll give the nurse my number too and we're not that much farther away than the hospital cafeteria. I'll wager the food is better at the bistro." He flashed the nurse an apologetic smile. "No offense."

She waved a hand. "Are you kidding? Given the choice, I'd choose the bistro every time."

While they were trying to convince Maeve to take a break, two additional nurses came in. They were dressed in dark-blue scrubs, with matching lab coats and cloth hats covering their hair. The taller of the two said, "Mr. Shepard, my name is Stu and I'll be your driver to the OR this afternoon, and this is Bridget. It's her job to make sure everyone gets out of our way."

Bridget moved to the side of the bed and looked at the hospital bracelet on his wrist and asked Henry his name, date of birth, the year, president, and if he knew what was about to happen. When he was finished reciting the answers for the second time in less than ten minutes, he asked, "Did I pass?"

Her fingers grazed the bedsheets near his arm. "With flying colors. Now, Mrs. Shepard, give your husband a kiss goodbye and the next time you see him, he'll be a little groggy but sporting some new hardware in his hip."

Leaning over the bed, she kissed him lightly on the mouth and whispered something only his dad could hear.

He brushed her cheek with his hand and gave her a loving smile.

"Enjoy lunch with Hank and I'll see you soon. I love you, sweetheart."

She kissed him again and this time her lips lingered on his. "I love you too, cowboy. Don't try and boss everyone around." She looked at Stu. "He thinks he's the boss, on or off the ranch."

Stu winked. "It's okay. We'll let him think he is until he gets the good drugs."

"See you, son." He held out his hand and Hank clasped it. Dad gave it a firm squeeze.

"I'll have a large black coffee for you, Pop."

"Make it two," he called out as the nurses eased the bed from its locked position and out the door.

Hank and his mom followed the nurses and his dad until they reached the elevator and backed the gurney inside the car. Once they were inside, his mom waved to his dad. "Love you, sweetheart."

He gave a thumbs-up as the doors closed. Hank opened his arms and wrapped them around his mom, providing all the comfort he could. Expecting a river of tears, he was surprised when she patted his chest.

"If we're going to the restaurant, you need to give the nurses your number. Then I want to hear everything that's going on with your life—and for the record, we're going to find a way for you and Renee to be in the same room without creating tension so thick a chainsaw wouldn't cut it."

"Yes, ma'am." He pointed over his shoulder. "I'll talk with the nurse at the desk and you get your handbag and coat." He wanted to get her out of there before she changed her mind.

*H*ank and his mom settled in a booth in the heart of the busy restaurant. She closed the menu and set it aside. "Before we order, I need for you to tell me one thing." She waved the waiter off.

It was never good when his mom waited to order. "Sure, what's that?"

She folded her hands on the tabletop and gave him the mom stare.

He wanted to squirm under her gaze like he had when he was a kid but there was no getting around whatever was to come next.

"Do you still have feelings for Renee Mitchell?"

"Mom, what kind of question is that?"

"Honest. Direct. Curious." She tipped her head to the side. "Your lack of an answer might be the answer I've suspected for a long time."

He leaned forward. "Mom, how do you stop loving the first person you gave your heart to?"

"I don't know since I married my first love." She placed her hand over his. "Is that all it is? First love? Or are there embers that could ignite for a more sustaining love?"

He looked out the window to the brick façade of the hospital, thinking how it felt when he saw Renee. His heart had soared and plummeted within seconds. "It doesn't matter. We've taken different paths in life, and when they crossed, like they did today, it didn't mean anything. We made our choices a long time ago." He could hear the regret in his voice, but it no longer held the bitterness he had harbored. Why wouldn't she agree to go to college closer to him? Or in hindsight, maybe he should have changed schools. There were good universities for prelaw, and then he could have gone to law school anywhere; it didn't have to be NYU for his undergrad work, even if it had been his dream school. He hadn't tried to find a way around the impasse. Selfish was the only word that sprang to mind.

"Hank." The sharp tone in Mom's voice drew him back to the present.

"What did you say?"

"I was agreeing you can't change the past but it's not like you have to live in Dallas. I happen to know that Robert Adler is thinking about retiring. Maybe you could take over his practice."

"I'm a defense lawyer, Mom. I don't do wills and house closings."

Her eyes grew wide and her mouth gaped open. "I can't believe you're so narrow-minded. There is a lot going on in River Junction and folks around here could use a top-notch attorney."

He sat up straighter. "Like what?"

"A developer is sniffing around, trying to buy up ranches to reimagine our little town into a tourist destination—and not the kind where locals co-exist with visitors. He wants to build fancy dude ranches that have less to do with raising cattle and more to do with pretending it's a ranch."

His gut tightened. "Have you and Dad been approached?"

"Of course. We've got a huge spread and Mr. Gasperini offered us a pretty penny, but we didn't think twice and turned him down flat. Your father still hopes that you and Ford will return home to run the ranch, preserving it for the next generation."

"I wish you had told me about Gasperini. I could send a letter telling him to back off."

"No need. Henry is formidable when it comes to his family's ranch. Besides, what would we have done with everyone who works for us? We couldn't just let them all go."

"Has anyone in town agreed to sell?"

"I'm not sure. The Mitchells turned him down last fall before Renee took over the orchard. Sara confided in me that she has already given Renee their blessing that if she wants to sell the land, she can. You know, if it proves too much for her. She lives in the big old house all alone."

That last sentence caused Hank to pay closer attention to what his mother was saying. "She's not involved with someone?"

"No. When she was over for dinner a few weeks back, I asked her if there was someone special but she laughed me off, saying she didn't have time to date. Her commitment was to the apples." She shook her head and made a *tsk-tsk* sound. "It's a shame. She's such a nice girl—and pretty too."

Hank stored all the new information to dissect later. "Mom, the orchard is just on the other side of the river from Stone's Throw. For a development company, Renee selling would be like opening the door to a candy store for a kid. Maybe we should offer to buy the orchard from her if she's looking to sell. Just to keep it out of the wrong hands."

"She's not interested." Mom winked and gave him a

knowing smile. "I knew you cared about River Junction."

"Of course I do. Just because I'm not packing my bags and moving back doesn't mean that I want to let some shady developer start buying up tracts of good ranch land to build a playground for people who want to pretend at being a cowboy."

The waiter cautiously approached their table and stopped a short distance away before asking, "Do you need a few more minutes with the menu?"

He said, "Yes. We haven't looked yet."

"Take your time and just give a wave when you're ready." She went to a nearby table and began chatting with a couple.

Mom opened the menu and glanced at him. "I never said the man was shady—persistent, yes. But there's nothing criminal about wanting to do his job, which is to buy land."

"There is if he's using pressure tactics." He tapped the tabletop with a butter knife. "Promise me, if this Mr. Gasperini comes back, you'll tell me right away. The last thing you and Pop need is added stress."

Mom flashed him a sweet smile. "Of course, son."

"Good." He withdrew his phone and tapped out a quick message to Ford. *Need to talk to you tonight. Stuff going on at the ranch you should know about.*

A quick reply came back. *I put Toby to bed at 8. Call any time after that. How long are you staying with the folks?*

I'm thinking a couple of weeks, see how the ranch is running, and I need to check on a few other things. We'll talk more tonight.

Hank looked up from his phone to see his mom watching him. "Ford and I are going to talk tonight. I thought Dad might want to say hello too." It was true. Too bad he just thought of that. "We should order. I'm starving." He held up his hand for the waitress and said, "What looks good, Mom?"

he snow had melted quickly over the last couple of weeks and now Renee stood in the middle of her newly planted field. The small apple trees that had taken her and the hired workers days to plant were trampled into the mud and the culprits grazed on the shoots of grass between the rows of what was to be the new section in her orchard. She threw her head back, fists balled at her sides, and let out an ear-splitting scream.

That helped her feel a smidge better—not that anyone could hear her since this was her orchard. Ginny had driven into Bozeman and the closest neighbor was a few miles away. She kicked a clod of dirt and muttered to herself as if she needed reminding. "Every day is critical; these trees need to take root, especially with the short growing season."

She was going to have to replace the stock. If it was even possible for her to get more. Then it would be at least a two-week setback and she was not calling her parents to vent the bad news. River Bend Orchard was her business now and she'd figure out a solution on her own. But first these stupid cows needed to get off her land before they did even more damage.

Taking slow, cautious steps, she inched closer to the large beasts, wary of how they might react. She paused and took slow, deep breaths to quiet her hammering heart. At least they didn't have those wide horns that were famous in Texas.

All these cows had yellow tags dangling from their ears as they moved, almost like earrings. Maybe the name of the ranch was stamped on them. She continued to creep closer so as not to spook them. When she was a foot or so away, she was disappointed to discover the tags had numbers, not even a ranch logo.

She popped her hands on her hips. "That's not going to do me a bit of good."

Reaching into her pocket for her cell phone, she paused and didn't bother to pull it out. Cell reception out there was spotty at best, and besides, who was she going to call? It's not like there was a local resource to help find lost cattle, was there?

On the other side of the winding riverbed, she noticed a lone figure galloping in her direction. At one time that might have been Hank, but it was probably just a ranch hand ready to drive the cows back across the river. She stomped over the now-downed trees, closing the distance between herself and the horse and rider.

A man was in the saddle.

She could tell he was tall but not who he was with his cowboy hat pulled low over his face, probably to keep the bright sun from his eyes. She thought about the fence she should have installed before planting for a fraction of a second, but now that the cows were out of the barn, there was no use worrying about that door being closed.

She lifted a hand in greeting and called out. "Missing any cows?"

He pulled up on the reins and the horse came to a full stop on the opposite side of the river. He scanned the landscape behind her and scowled. "As a matter of fact, I am and I can see they've invaded your orchard."

Her heart sank. She knew that deep, smooth voice and taking a better look, the way he sat astride the horse was burned into a long-forgotten memory, until now. Renee dismissed the way her heart skittered in her chest. She needed to stick to the business at hand and have Hank drive his cows back across the river. If they crossed once, they could do it again; thankfully the water wasn't running high or fast.

"Yes, they did. We need to discuss the damage they caused to my trees."

Hank urged his horse through the water, and it danced up the low-rise bank in front of her.

He swung his leg over the back of the saddle and jumped down before giving her a hard look. A flicker of amusement flashed in his caramel-brown eyes, but it was gone just as quickly.

Renee took a step back and stumbled. Before she landed on her butt, he took her by the arm and steadied her.

"Renee, are you alright?"

The deep timbre of his voice caused her stomach to become a hive of honeybees buzzing around the buttercups in spring. Hank Shepard was the first boy she had ever kissed and the one man she couldn't forget no matter how hard she tried. Other than a touch of gray at the temples of his light-brown hair and the deep crinkles around his eyes, he looked exactly the same—drop-dead gorgeous as ever. It would have been better if he'd gotten out of shape with a big belly, but no—he had stayed trim and muscular. But she already knew this after their quick run-in at the hospital a few weeks back.

"Renee?"

Despite the way his voice made her belly flip, she had to focus on the question and not the man asking it.

"Yes, I'm fine. I just tripped on a root."

He looked down at the grassy bank and gave her a quirk of a smile. "Glad it wasn't anything bigger."

She wanted to groan but there wasn't much else to say about the root that wasn't any thicker than a strand of spaghetti. "So, about your cows." She couldn't help but notice he still held her arm. The warmth of his hand penetrated her fleece. She took a step back to break their connection. It was the only way she could think clearly.

"They're not really mine, not anymore. I'm still helping Dad out, you know, running things until he's back in the saddle, literally. I'll be heading back to Dallas soon, doing my lawyer thing again."

It was funny how he slipped that in, and there went the idea of suing the cows for damages. She laughed—suing cows.

"What's funny, me being a lawyer or living in Dallas?" He gave her a long look just like he did when they were kids and he was trying to figure out what she was thinking.

"It's nothing other than we need to talk about the damage done to my orchard. I just planted new tree stock last week and now your cows"—she jerked her thumb over her shoulder—"your dad's cows walked all over them like it was the yellow brick road."

"It might not be that bad; do you mind if I take a look?"

With a sweeping gesture in the direction of the expansive field, she said, "See for yourself."

He looked from side to side. "Where's the fencing?"

She kicked the ground with the toe of her work boot. "On order. It should be here in a few days." Which was the least of her problems. Once it was delivered, she didn't know how she would afford to hire men to get it installed. She had resigned herself to setting posts and was more than capable, given that she had done it many times with her dad, even if it was years ago. Fingers crossed that it would be muscle memory; the know-how would just come back to her.

If he sensed she was holding back, he didn't show it. With a curt nod, he said, "Care to lead the way?"

With his horse plodding behind him, Hank followed Renee as she crossed the section of field that hadn't been planted, at least not this year.

She held back the tears that threatened to roll down her cheeks when she stepped around the tiny green leaves crushed into the dirt, the light-brown sticks, split like strands of spaghetti, jutted from the ground. The analogy was the best she could up with, and since pasta was Hank's favorite, it was okay to compare the damage to Italian food.

"Renee, I'm really sorry about the mess. Get me the estimate of the damage and I'll cut you a check so you can buy new trees."

That was nice but he didn't understand; it wasn't just the trees. She'd need to turn over the soil again, prep the bare root stock, and replant. She was looking at a couple more weeks of work and then the fence on top of that.

"I can do that." She looked at the cows contentedly munching on what was left of her field, and not that she was counting, but there had to be at least fifty of them. On the upside, any cow patties left behind were free fertilizer.

Who was she kidding? That wasn't much of a consolation prize.

He pulled his billfold out of his front jeans pocket and handed her a business card. "My email address is on the front. Just send over the cost and I'll drop off a check tomorrow if you're going to be home."

"Yeah, sure. I'll probably be out here so you can just leave it in the mailbox." She'd have to hook up the plow to get the rows churned up again. But at least she could get the stock on order tonight and the land would be ready when it arrived. Then again, maybe she could expedite the shipment too; after all, how much could that cost?

She gave Hank a steady look. Maybe she'd just slide the air freight charges into the price of the trees so he'd have to pay for it. But she quickly dismissed that idea. That was dishonest, and they had been friends once upon a time. She wouldn't do that to an enemy, let alone a former friend.

He gave her that wide smile that she remembered so well.

"I'll drive these girls across the river. Don't forget to email me." He looked over the field. "And I'm real sorry about all of this, but you should get the fence installed before you plant again."

Yeah, yeah, yeah, she should do a lot of things and if she ever got to that to-do list she wrote out for herself, she'd be organized and already prepared for fall harvest. As it was, she hadn't even had time to look over the list and start with what she had thought was the number one priority. Not that she'd admit any of that to Hank. As far as he was concerned, she was the businesswoman of the year in River Junction—well, maybe the orchard businesswoman of the year at a bare minimum.

She forced a bright smile. "It's at the top of my list."

"Good." He stuck his left boot in the stirrup and settled into the saddle like a cowboy ready to work the herd. She thought it was ironic since that was what he'd been born into. Instead, he'd traded in his Levi's and Stetson for a suit and tie.

He gave a sharp whistle, and the cows slowly raised their heads while he wove his horse through the herd. Once he got to the farthest cow, he began to urge them in her direction. She moved off to one side and was surprised. It looked like he had been doing it forever, instead of leaving

Montana after graduation, never to return except for quick holiday trips.

Who was she to judge? Hadn't she done the same thing? College, graduation, and then settled in Chicago. At least her plan had always been to make enough money so that someday she'd return home and run the family business. Once, when they were young, Hank said when he left, he wasn't ever living in Small Town, USA again but she hadn't believed him.

As he rode past her, he tipped his hat and gave her a saucy wink. "See you tomorrow, Renee. And by the way, you're looking pretty as always." He tapped his spurs to the sides of his horse and finished pushing the herd to the edge of the water before splashing across.

She watched until the cowboy and the cattle were tiny moving specs, headed to Stone's Throw Ranch. She had to wonder how long he would be in town.

He had said he was leaving soon.

Maybe they could get together for coffee or something— just for old times' sake, of course. She crossed the dirt path where her bicycle leaned against a fence post. She'd best get back to the house and dig up the paperwork and then source new tree stock. She was counting on the new apple trees to produce in a couple of years. If she was going to make a viable business of the orchard, she needed to expand and produce a line of products to sell at tourist stores all across the state. And if that went well, she was thinking of other kinds of fruit trees she could plant and expand the business even more.

She glanced over her shoulder and could picture the orchard, lush with a riot of delicate white and pink apple flower buds. There was nothing like Montana in the spring.

8

*A*fter bumping into Renee at the hospital, he had almost given up hope of seeing her before he left. He turned in the saddle to catch one last glimpse of her. *Cows. Who would have thought cows would have given me a second chance to see her again?* It had been years since he allowed those old feelings to bubble to the surface. And now, despite telling his mother there was nothing between them, he knew it was a lie. All he wanted was to hold her close and actually feel her in his arms instead of only in his dreams.

The lowing cattle drew his attention away from thoughts of their past. He would purchase the new tree stock after the Shepard cows trampled her orchard. It was the least he could do—and he'd help her replant. By the looks of the empty field, she was the only one working that day.

He clucked his tongue and Ranger, his horse, trotted forward. He needed to erase his first impulse, to take her in his arms and kiss her just to satisfy his curiosity to see whether their bodies still fit together like peanut butter and bread.

Hank drove the herd at a steady pace to the paddock and once he secured them, he'd round up a couple of hands to ride the fence line and fix any other spots where the cattle might escape. If there was one place there could be more. Replanting the apple trees wasn't going to be a successful long-term solution since the cows found an easy way to get to the other side of the river unless she installed fencing soon.

With a snort, he thought, *Maybe the grass is greener on the other side.*

Once the plan was in action, he'd swing by the house and ask his dad about Renee's financial situation. She seemed a bit prickly when it came to him covering the cost of the trees. *Or maybe it was my imagination. But she got defensive when I offered her money for gas too. Pop always has had his finger on the pulse of the happenings in River Junction.*

As Hank rode back to the barn at an easy trot, he kept an eye out for Joe. He spotted him going into the office and gave a sharp whistle to get Joe's attention. Hank squeezed his legs into Ranger's sides urging him into a canter.

"Joe," he shouted, "we've got a problem in the south pasture next to the river across from River Bend Orchard."

"What's that, Hank?"

He pushed his cowboy hat back and rubbed his eyes. "The fence is down and part of the herd crossed the river. The water was pretty shallow there which, was a good thing—we didn't lose a steer, but we'll need to get that fence fixed before we use the pasture again. Can you round up a few hands and take care of that today?"

"Ya got it, boss." He tapped the brim of his cowboy hat and sauntered in the direction of the barn.

· · ·

*a*fter taking care of Ranger and giving him an extra helping of oats, Hank made his way to the main house. The kitchen door banged closed behind him and he called out, "Hey, Pop," and headed in the direction of the den. It had become his dad's favorite room since the hip surgery.

Once he and Ford left home, Mom had turned their playroom into a man cave, complete with a large-screen television that rivaled those in most sports bars.

"Hank, back here."

His dad was reclining in his chair with a book in his hand when Hank walked in, his walker within arm's reach. He put the book he had been reading on the side table and gave Hank a welcoming smile. It was like looking into the future by thirty years; they had the same smile, dimple, and eyes.

Hank perched on the edge of the dark-brown leather sofa, another new addition to the space. "Pop, around fifty head of our cattle got out and found their way across that creek—you know, the one that's out past the south pasture."

His dad frowned. "Any get swept away?"

"No, the water is pretty low. I'm guessing there's a beaver dam upstream which is good in this instance, since they crossed into River Bend Orchard and had a field day. Pun intended."

He frowned. "That doesn't sound good; how much damage?"

Not that he thought Renee would sue them, but he should have taken pictures with his cell to show his dad. "It's pretty bad. They took out the entire new field of tree stock. I bumped into Renee and she's pretty shook up. I didn't see any workers around when I was over there."

"Yeah, she took over last fall and from what Dave

Mitchell said, she is aggressive with her expansion plans. Talk in town is, money's tight over there. She's planning on buying industrial kitchen equipment, wanting to expand into selling more apple products—not just the fruit and cider. I'm going to assume to reach her goal she's planting a wider variety." He drummed his fingertips on the arm of his chair. "Did she mention if she's got the same crew of orchard workers she had last year?"

"What are you talking about?" Hank knew most people didn't change jobs like the wind in River Junction. When you found a good job, you hung on to it, and you either fell in love with the area or you didn't. There were no two ways about it.

"I guess you didn't hear; the orchard's had some tough times. I think that's why she moved back from Chicago and took over. Your mom said she was some big shot interior designer. Dave's health hasn't been the best. And then two years ago, they lost their blossoms to a late spring snowstorm. Mother Nature's fickle for any farmer and it doesn't matter if you're raising cows or chickens or vegetables and fruits, bad weather never helps your bottom line."

"Yeah, I know that we've had many a tight year—but Dad, somehow you always manage to find a way to make it work."

His mom came through the archway carrying a tray with three mugs and a plate piled high with cookies. The coffee teased his nose, but the cookies made his mouth water. This was something he'd missed, his favorite chocolate chip cookie. If he had one weakness, it'd be cookies with lots of dark chocolate chunks and walnuts. He got up and took the tray from her. "Thanks, Mom, but I would have come into the kitchen for this."

"It wasn't any bother. I was bringing some in to your dad, and this way you'll stay for a few minutes and fill me in on what's been going on before you get busy again. I know there are a lot of hours still left in the day and you won't be back until suppertime."

He took a bite of a cookie and groaned. "Mom, you definitely know how to spoil your favorite son."

She gave him a lopsided grin. "It's a good thing your brother is out of town; he'd be wrestling you for those cookies and that title of favorite."

His dad cleared his throat as Hank passed him a mug of coffee and set the plate on the side table. "Maeve, we were just talking about Renee's orchard. Seems our cattle made a mess of that new field she mentioned planting."

"Oh no. That poor girl, she just can't catch a break." She settled next to his dad in the matching recliner.

Hank sipped his coffee. He was anxious to get the lowdown on what was going on with Renee, but peppering his parents with questions was bound to raise suspicions as to why he wanted to know.

His mom said, "Hank, ranching is different than farming. We can recover more easily when there is a setback with nature. Apple blossoms are fragile like newborn babies. Without that initial nurturing, there isn't a harvest—and there's nothing you can do about Mother Nature."

"Yeah, you've been saying that all my life, but our cows damaged her new root stock so I'm going to replace it. For the record, I'm not expecting it to come out of the ranch budget. Renee needs help and I intend on helping her."

His dad said, "Son, you're a good man and I wouldn't expect anything less, but the ranch can cover the cost." He arched a brow. "Is there something more to this situation than just being neighborly? Any chance some of those old feelings surfaced now that you've seen her a couple of times?"

Out of the corner of his eye, Hank noticed his mom had leaned forward in her chair. It was obvious she was interested in his answer even if she hadn't interjected yet. It had always been her way to let his dad do most of the talking—not that she didn't have an opinion, because she always did.

He hated that he was about to lie to them. "It was nice to see her but there are zero twinges. I'm sure there's not much of those old feelings left to resurrect—and besides, Renee has probably long since moved on." *Who am I trying to convince, my parents or me? Who have I become? The Cowardly Lion? I can't admit to them there's a part of me that misses her and what we had.*

His dad dunked a cookie in his coffee. "Well, I happen to know she's single." He looked at Hank over the rim of the mug and winked.

So now he understood where this was going.

His dad was attempting to play matchmaker.

"That doesn't mean I can hang around River Junction. I have a law practice waiting for me and I'll be leaving once you're released to work."

"You do, but you know what they say, son; once Montana gets in your blood, it never leaves."

His dad stopped talking as his mom said, "Henry, stop. You promised. No pressure during Hank's visit."

He appreciated his mom speaking up, but it wasn't necessary. Montana would always be a part of him. There was something about the land and the ranch that caused his heart to beat at a slow and steady pace the minute he drove under the wooden arch. But he had a life in Dallas. How was he supposed to pick up and move back to the ranch and throw away all those years of law school? It wasn't like he could practice law in River Junction since there wasn't a need for defense attorneys out in these parts.

"Thanks for the reminder, Pop." He settled back on the sofa.

His dad looked up from his coffee cup and gave Hank a

sharp look. "Son, do you know specifically where the cattle crossed the stream onto her land?"

He liked that his dad wasn't about to dwell on Hank's last comment and moved back to Renee's situation. "Yes, and Joe already sent some men out to repair it. But it wasn't just that they got on her land. Based on what was left of the root stock, they couldn't have been more than three feet tall. You know what a nine-hundred-plus-pound cow can do to land when they graze."

"I know all that and you're right." He turned to his wife. "Let your mother know how much it costs to replace the trees. When it comes down to the bottom line, Stone's Throw Ranch meets their obligations. It's not right that you pay for the replacements. Besides, neighbors help neighbors around here and it's not just about helping other cattle folk. Farms are just as important to River Junction."

He admired his parents. They were hardworking people and they had their share of rough times in the past, but they had always found a way to support their friends and neighbors.

"I'm gonna head out. Thanks for the shot of caffeine and sugar, Mom. I'll check to make sure that fence is fixed and see you at dinner." He picked up his hat but didn't place it on his head. "I want to make sure the cattle don't find their way back across the stream."

"What about the rest of the fence line?" His dad inched his way to the edge of his chair with a grunt and dragged his walker toward him. He heaved himself up with a grimace and swayed from side to side before he settled. Henry Shepard was a proud and stubborn man and Hank waited in case he needed help but did not want to offer it prematurely.

"I'll make sure the entire fence line is inspected. It'll take a while, but again, we need to keep our neighbors' property safe. Besides, that river's fast in spots and we don't wanna lose any of the herd."

"Have them check for a dam too. It's odd, with spring thaw. That water should be running fast and high." He gave a sharp nod. "I look forward to hearing what you find out."

His mom got to her feet, her arm resting on his dad's hand. "Dear, you should be taking it easy."

"I'm bored to tears. If there was a way I could get on a horse, I'd be out there riding the darn fence line—if nothing else than for a change of scenery."

"I'll take pictures, Dad. Will that help you feel in the loop?"

He patted Hank's shoulder. "Thanks, and in case I forgot to tell you, I really appreciate you coming home to help out. I know you're anxious to get back to the city and your practice. I'm hoping the doctor releases me back to work when I meet with her next week."

"Don't push it, Dad. I'll stay as long as you need."

*L*ater that night, after dinner and a hot shower, Hank reclined on his bed, checking his work email. He wanted to stay on top of his cases and when he saw there was an email from River Bend Orchard, a smile filled his face. He scanned the contents and then went back to read it again before looking at the attachment. Renee was nothing if not thorough. She attached a scan of the recent invoice where she had made notations about the extra fertilizer she used and what she needed for other enhancements to give the trees a boost, but there was nothing to indicate the price of labor to plant. He knew it would cost her overtime for people to replant and he also knew, based on what his dad said, her budget might be tight. Why hadn't she accounted for labor?

Tomorrow when he took the check over, he'd ask about the labor expense cost and see if there was something more he could do. His dad had taught him to always pay it forward, help out your neighbors—but in this case, it was more than that. He wanted to help out an old friend.

He got off the twin bed and crossed to the window. Shadows had lengthened as he surveyed the expanse of the ranch. The moon was high in the sky and in the distance the mountains loomed like sentries guarding the valley. Was there something more to his desire to help Renee, like his dad insinuated? They had been best friends and then high school sweethearts. By Thanksgiving their freshman year, it was apparent they had drifted apart. He dropped his head and turned from the view that had often given him peace. He would help her get the trees replaced. It'd be much easier for him to go back to pretending Renee Mitchell didn't exist. Because living on Stones Throw Ranch with her just next door and not being with her was the second hardest thing he'd ever had to do.

he morning after the cattle had destroyed her trees, Renee had been awake before the birds to tinker with the tractor's engine in an attempt to get it to turn over. A few hours later, as she was perched on the thin cushioned seat, she looked to the sky as she turned the key. "Please let this work." It sputtered and choked on heaven only knew what, then died again. But from past experience, she just needed to wait it out and if all went well, the engine would soon be running as smooth as silk.

After several minutes she turned the key again; this time the engine purred. She dropped the transmission into low gear and puttered in the direction of the field. Since she was finally moving, there wasn't any rush.

With her hands lightly clasped around the wheel she rolled her shoulders; she figured it was easier to let go of all the things she couldn't control even though the last thing she wanted to do was rework a field. Facing the task annoyed her, but it had to be done and she was the only person who could do it. She reached the edge of the field and with a flick of the gear switch, she lowered the plow into the dark—almost black—soil. Defeat washed over her as the tractor lumbered forward. The plow bit into the soil and churned the first never-ending row. She drove up and down the length of the field, back and forth, losing count early on. With any luck she'd finish by dinner.

As she drove under the warm spring sun, her thoughts turned to what was left of the current root stock. She had picked through what the cattle had left, grateful she could save twenty trees. But that number wasn't going to breathe new life into her orchard. She didn't know how she was going to get the new stock planted either. Already over budget and with every penny counted twice, she'd have to enlist Ginny's help because she couldn't afford to hire the workers again.

By noon, she needed to take a break. She parked the tractor near the barn and crossed the gravel drive. Her heart was heavy and once inside the old farmhouse, she poured a large glass of cold water from the pitcher in the icebox. *Does anyone even call it an icebox anymore?* The quiet was unnerving; she hoped Ginny would be back that night. She could use someone to talk to about the obstacles looming—not to solve her problems but to act as a sounding board. Her beloved kitty, Smokey, pretty much slept all the time and although he was a good listener, his advice was lacking.

As she stood in front of the sink, a newer pickup truck parked next to the house. The door bore the logo of the Stone's Throw Ranch. *What is going on?* Was Henry okay? She hurried outside, stopping on the top step of the back porch.

Lo and behold, there was Hank Shepard, looking handsome as ever with that swagger in his walk. He raised his hand in greeting and gave her that familiar heart-fluttering smile.

"Hey, Renee." He reached the stairs and rested one foot

on the lower step. He leaned forward. "What's the good word today?"

"Is Henry okay?"

"Sure. I wanted to stop by personally to check in. So, what are you up to?"

She exhaled a sigh of relief. "Oh, you know, just working. Farming is a lot like ranching. Get up with the sun, work, work, and more work. Take a break, then work some more, break for lunch, and repeat for the afternoon." She hoped her voice didn't sound as weary as she felt. The last thing she needed was for Hank to feel sorry for her.

He held out a nondescript white envelope which she figured held the check. But her heart sank a little. The money would help but how was she going to get the new tree stock there fast enough to be planted during the optimal window? When she checked online, everything she wanted was backordered by a month. She forced a tight smile to her lips and took the envelope. "Thanks, I appreciate this."

"You're welcome but it was our cattle who trampled your trees and made a mess of your field so it's the least we can do. And heck, if your apples had made a mess of my cattle, I'd be expecting some sort of payment in return."

She couldn't help but feel a real smile gracing her lips at his lame attempt to lighten the situation. "Thanks. You always knew how to take something and twist it to your advantage." What she didn't say was he always knew how to make her laugh and obviously that hadn't changed. "I'll make sure to keep my unruly apples out of your field."

A deep, unrestrained laugh bubbled up from deep inside him. "Heck, the cows would love your apples; they'd be like sweet, delicious, juicy treats for them. After all, look how much they enjoyed the trees."

"I thought you'd send over the check with a ranch hand and not deliver it personally." *Why is he standing here making small talk?* She had a ton of work to do. But she wasn't going to get snarky with him; after all, he did pay for the damage.

He casually looked around. She noticed the way his eyes narrowed and seemed to pause as he looked toward Tony's truck in the parking area, his toolbox open on the tailgate. For a few uncomfortable moments, she wanted to throw the envelope back to him, but that was her pride talking and it would be downright foolish. As much as she hated to take the money, she knew she had no other choice; her credit cards were maxed and a bank loan wasn't a viable option either.

"I appreciate you stopping over. Let your parents know this fall, apples are on me."

He straightened up. "I'll be sure to tell them, and you know, Renee, I was thinking." He looked at his watch and back to her.

"Uh-oh. If I remember correctly, that was never a good sign when we were kids—the, 'I was thinking' phrase." She held his gaze.

"No, this is good." He held up the Scout's salute. "Promise." He pointed to the envelope. "Why don't you open that."

"I'll do that later. I really need to get back to work."

He looked in the direction of the tractor. "Plowing up the rows?"

It felt like a hive of bees began fluttering in her gut— the buzzing spread through her chest and was ready to explode through her limbs. An old, familiar sign he was beginning to annoy her. *I don't have time to be jaw-jacking when there is work to do.* She crossed her arms over her midsection and scuffed the toe of her work boot against the dark green painted porch floor.

He reached out and flicked the edge of the envelope. "Do me a favor and open it."

She hated when anyone pushed her, but if it would get him off her land quicker, she might just as well. She ripped open one end and a paper fluttered to the ground. She picked it up. It wasn't a check.

She could feel the color drain from her face. It was an IOU. *How am I going to buy tree stock with a slip of worthless paper?* She had ten acres to plant, most of which the cows had destroyed.

Holding the slip of paper in her hand, she blinked away the tears stinging her eyes. I— I don't understand." There was no crying in business—especially not in front of an old boyfriend.

"When I looked over what you needed to reorder last night, I checked several nurseries online that stocked similar to what you purchased on the original order. They were all sold out for at least a month."

Heat spread up her neck and across her cheeks, setting up camp there as her temper spiked. *How dare he poke his nose into my business; I didn't ask him to do anything like that.*

She looked in the direction of the field, took a couple of slow breaths, and rubbed her temples as a low-level headache crept in. "Not to worry, I'll find replacement stock. I have some feelers out and I should have something by the weekend."

He gave her that heart-melting smile again. She was annoyed to discover her heart hadn't completely crusted over from the pain of losing him. It flickered a couple of extra beats and she wanted to give him a chance to explain the IOU.

"That's what I wanted to tell you. I found semi-dwarf tree stock and it will deliver this afternoon. They're bought and paid for too."

"Hank." Why hadn't he discussed this with her first? Her parents had always planted full-size trees; how would that work? "There are different requirements for how many trees per acre between different sizes—dwarf, semi, and standard."

"Ree, you need to trust me on this. I did the research and I ordered enough for a little over three acres. It was all the supplier had, but he'll ship more in a few days."

She ignored the use of her nickname. "How did you even know the acreage I'm planting?"

He shifted from one foot to the other and grinned. "You make great margin notes. All I had to do was remember your special shorthand and placing the order was a snap."

Her heart constricted; it was a sweet gesture. "You didn't need to go to all the trouble." If she didn't have sad, lingering emotions from their breakup, this might have turned the tide in his favor. He was still the good guy she remembered even if he had broken her heart—or to be fair, they had broken each other's hearts—not that she was about to admit it.

He touched the brim of his tattered high school baseball cap and with a twinkle in his eye, he said, "No trouble at all, ma'am."

Now she couldn't help but let out a good belly laugh. "The Texas drawl does suit you."

"Thank ya kindly. Now if you wouldn't mind a little help, I'd be more than willing to plant a few trees after they arrive."

She could tell her smile faded as his expression dimmed. "I'm fine, Hank. I've got good people to help me." The lie died on her lips.

The people she hired moved from job to job. They'd come back but at a higher price per hour and she had her dwindling bank account to consider. *If I can get the plowing done today, I can start planting tomorrow and semi-dwarf trees would be easier for me and Ginny to handle.* With a little luck, she'd be finished with the first three acres in a few days— just in time for the rest of the trees to arrive.

He took one more look around but didn't call her on the bluff. "It's a standing offer and I've got time to help. So don't hesitate to ask."

"I appreciate that. I'm fine but I'll let you know when the truck arrives, and after I inventory the trees, just to let you know everything's all set."

He nodded. "Then I'll head back over to the ranch. Maybe we could grab a cup of coffee and a slice of pie at the Filler Up Diner. Mom mentioned Maggie still makes one heck of a pie, even if it's not huckleberry season."

She longed to say yes as fast as the words would come out of her mouth but instead, she said, "Maybe."

His smile didn't fade this time. "See you around, Renee. And remember to call if you need anything—anything at all."

"Thanks, Hank—and tell your mom and dad I said hello."

A wave of loneliness swept over her as he got in his truck. She watched as he did a wide turn in the middle of the drive before lifting his hand in a final wave. It had been good to see him, even for a few fleeting minutes. Those old feelings she had buried long ago pushed against the tiny crack in her heart. If she weren't careful, it would bust wide open. She waited until he was farther down the drive before she returned the wave. Not that he was looking in the rearview mirror. *I'm just the girl from his youth, and he must have a wonderful woman in Dallas*. Nice guys like Hank always had someone special.

After she checked on Tony, who was still tinkering with the cider press, she'd jump back on the tractor. Plowing didn't get done just thinking about it, and with another few hours, she could make a huge dent in the task, even though she had hoped to finish. After that she needed to do some research on semi-dwarf trees; was there anything different she'd need to do for staking them or soil enhancements?

. . .

*J*t had been a long day bouncing around on the worn seat of the old tractor and unloading the new trees. Renee walked out of the bathroom, wrapped in a cozy terrycloth robe, rubbing a hand towel over her hair. She sat down at her desk and reread the webpage she found regarding her new trees.

Hank had not only bought new stock, but the variety interested her most. It was well suited for cider and other preserves. It was as if he remembered a long-ago conversation when she mentioned she wanted to expand further into that part of the business. She had shared many of her dreams for the orchard while they lay in the back of his truck bed on long summer nights, watching the stars.

Hank had dreamed of becoming a lawyer and his dream became a reality.

She wanted to be a grower but went to design school to make money to buy the orchard from her parents. They both had realized their dreams.

She glanced at a framed photo on her desk; it was the last photo of them at the river with a group of school friends before everyone left for college. They'd promised to not let the real world drive a wedge between them, but that was naïve and things happened. Maybe she should have packed away the photos her mom had left sitting out, but the memories were bittersweet—and as time went by, it was more sweet than bitter.

Her cell rang. She didn't bother to look at the screen, assuming it was her mom as there wasn't anyone else she expected to hear from.

"Hello, Mom."

A deep, soft chuckle caressed her ears. She remembered that laugh, letting it wrap around her like a warm hug.

"It's Hank."

"Hello. This is unexpected."

"I was waiting for you to call and when you didn't, I wanted to make sure you got the delivery. I checked the tracking and it said the trees arrived."

She shook her head, silently admonishing herself. After all, she had promised to call and didn't. "I'm sorry, Hank. The stock looks strong. Thank you for arranging everything. It was above and beyond."

"Good, I'm glad. Are you planting tomorrow?"

She pressed a hand to her lower back, stiff from bouncing over ten acres on the tractor, and tomorrow would be even worse after lifting and bending all day. "That's the plan."

"It should be good weather—and you can rest assured, the cattle won't make a return visit. The fence has been fixed and the hands checked the entire fence line."

She smiled into the phone. With a laugh, she said, "Good to know. Well, thanks for calling."

"Shout if you need anything. I'm only as far away as a few taps on your phone."

She didn't want to end the conversation. It was like the old days; Hank's quick wit about mundane details had a way of making her laugh in all situations.

"Thanks again for finding the new stock." She knew she was repeating herself but talking with him had thrown her off her game. "Even though these trees won't bear fruit for a couple of years, it's still..." Would he understand a good day at the orchard was gold?

"I get it. Life in Montana isn't for the faint of heart and we have to make use of each good day before the cold and snow settles back in."

Ranch life wasn't much different than farm life in that part of the country but there wasn't any place she'd rather be.

He said, "Before you go, do you know who might have built a dam farther up the creek that divides our land?"

"No. I didn't know there was one, but that explains why the water's been so low the last year. Have beavers or debris collected over the last few spring thaws and slowed things down or do you think it was man made?"

"Definitely not Mother Nature. It has structure to it. Not to worry, I'm going to talk with my dad and we'll let you know when we're going to dismantle it. The water is needed for the cattle and your orchard."

"Why would someone do that?"

Hank paused. "I'm not sure since the land on both sides of the river belongs to you and me."

She made a mental note to ask her father too. "I'm glad you found the issue and thanks for telling me."

"You're welcome."

She stifled a yawn. "I've got a busy day ahead of me so have a good night. And Hank, you're a good friend."

"It takes one to know one, Renee. Sleep well."

She didn't get up from the chair, mulling over the news about the dam and her conversation with Hank until a chill stole over her. With one last look at a younger Hank and his smile, she shut off the desk lamp.

———————

10

*T*he next morning when Hank woke, Renee was his first thought. The nagging idea she needed help but was too proud to ask weighed heavy on his mind. Yesterday when he was at her orchard, he heard someone working in one of the barns, but it didn't seem to be focused on planting with the tractor sitting in the driveway.

He dressed in a pair of Levi's, a short-sleeved tee, and a plaid flannel shirt. Then he followed the tantalizing aroma of fresh-brewed coffee and went into the kitchen where his parents were chatting over a cup.

"Morning," he said as he poured a mug of steaming coffee, his stomach grumbling. Nothing like hard work the day before to wake up ravenous in the morning. "I'm going to get my chores done early and then head over to the Mitchell place."

His mom got up from the table. "Let me get your plate for you. Breakfast is already fixed and on the sideboard."

He placed a hand on her shoulder. "I appreciate the gesture but no need to wait on me." He flicked back the napkin on the plate she pointed to and discovered a mound of scrambled eggs and fat sausage links with an oversized corn muffin for good measure. The meal would hit the spot and stick to his ribs. He dragged the chair across the old linoleum floor and before he took a seat, he said, "Anyone need a refill on coffee?"

"No, thanks." His dad leveled a look at him. "What are you going to do at the Mitchell farm?"

Hank added a liberal dose of hot sauce to his eggs and buttered his muffin—and as an afterthought added a dollop of his mom's homemade apple butter.

"When I stopped by yesterday it was like a ghost town over there. Someone had used the tractor; it had fresh clumps of dirt on the plow blade. I'm guessing it was Renee. Except for some banging coming from the barn, I didn't see another soul. I got the impression she's going to plant the trees by herself and that's more than any one person can handle, no matter how stubborn they are."

His mom gave him a knowing smile. "You always did have a tender spot for that girl—all the way back to grade school."

She wasn't wrong but it wasn't the time to admit it. "It's the neighborly thing to do, so I'll check in with Joe before I head out and make sure he's all set. I can't stand the thought of her working alone when I can lend some muscle."

"You're probably right." His dad nodded his approval which made the conversation a little easier. "You should take a couple of men with you."

That was a very generous offer from his dad. "That might be the right thing to do. I ordered close to six hundred trees."

His brows knitted together. "Isn't that too many?" he asked.

"When I talked to the customer service person at the wholesale nursery, they said you can actually put anywhere from one to three hundred per acre—so I split the difference."

His dad's brow shot up. "Did our cattle damage six hundred trees?"

"Not exactly, but I couldn't get the full-sized variety, so I bought enough to plant the field they were in." He shoveled some eggs into his mouth. The conversation was beginning to probe a little too deep and there were unasked questions he didn't want to face. Like why he hadn't just replaced the exact number of trees that were damaged. Hank admired Renee's gutsiness to expand, and this was the only way he could support her vision.

He steered the conversation to driving the cattle to higher ground for grazing and swayed from the topic of a certain pretty redhead with velvety-brown eyes. After putting his dishes in the dishwasher, he kissed the top of his mom's head and said he'd touch base before he took off.

*H*ank parked in front of one of the brick-red barns that bore the River Bend Orchard logo. It was a bit weathered but still stood out to welcome people who came to pick apples each fall. He glanced around as he strode to the house. The only sounds he heard were birds chirping, and the parking lot was devoid of vehicles in what he guessed was the employee lot. In addition, there were pallets of root stock placed around the area too but no tractor. His hunch was starting to look correct.

He rapped on the glass pane in the kitchen door. The midmorning sun was rising higher in the cloudless blue sky. He hadn't expected anyone to answer but logically it was the best place to start.

He got back in his truck and drove in the direction of the field. He glanced at the cooler on the passenger seat; he'd stopped to pack water and sandwiches, enough for both of them, along with a container of cookies fresh from the oven, courtesy of his mom.

The truck bounced along the rutted lane, highlighting the need for fresh gravel, at least in the deepest holes. It was a wonder she didn't break a tractor axel, but then again, she probably knew right where they were and drove around them. Well, he'd know for next time too.

His arm rested in the open window, enjoying the simple pleasure before thoughts turned to when he'd head back to Dallas—that was as soon as Dad was mobile. *There might not be another time I'll drive down this lane.*

When he took a left turn, he saw the tractor in the distance hooked to a flatbed trailer loaded to the edges with trees. He scanned the area and saw one person up ahead. He gripped the steering wheel and tamped down the annoyance. Why hadn't she asked for help? Stubborn pride. That was the reason he'd work right alongside her and get it done—and for his pay, he was taking her out for pie. *Maybe not tonight but soon.*

He parked the truck under a large apple tree, its canopy filled with blossoms, and got out. If nothing else, it looked like this year's harvest was promising. He watched as she climbed onto the tractor and headed in his direction. After several minutes, she slowed and came to a stop.

Perched in the seat, she gave him a tight smile. "Hank, what are you doing here? Don't you have something that needs your attention at the ranch? Like fixing fences, roping cattle, annoying the hands?"

He shrugged and made sure a wide grin was plastered on his face, one he hoped was irresistible. "As a matter of fact, I'm free and thought I might keep you company, being neighborly and all."

She gave him the stink eye —the one where she crossed her arms over her midsection and tilted her head down, eyes narrowed. It nearly took his breath away. He hadn't realized until that moment how much he missed this woman and all her moods.

"If I had wanted your help, I would have asked when we talked last night."

He took a few steps in her direction. "Are you saying you have so much help you can't use an extra pair of hands?"

That was one way to challenge her without stating the obvious.

"I have people."

He pointed to the pile of fencing and then the tree stock. "You got a lot going on here." Not that he would mention it, but both of these jobs were time consuming which equaled expensive. If things were as tight as he thought, she'd do it alone no matter how long it took.

"Ginny'll be back tomorrow and she's going to pitch in."

"Ginny from college?"

She thrust her chin up and glared at him.

But he'd poke the bear a bit more. Two people couldn't plant this field quickly.

"Yes, she left Chicago and is staying here for a couple of weeks. But she had to go out of town for a few days. Work. So don't you worry, I've got everything covered."

"I'm sure you do but I've got guys standing around and they need to keep busy so I'd like to bring them over to pitch in. You can oversee all of us."

Her shoulders drooped and he could only guess the burden she carried. He softened his voice, "Look, I get it. You've taken over the orchard and we both understand it's a hard and fickle business. Accepting help for something you had zero control over doesn't mean you're any less capable. It shows your willingness to put your personal feelings aside for the sake of your business."

"I don't know…" She looked across the newly plowed field.

"Renee, if I was in a tight spot, would you help me?"

She gave him an appraising look as if she were measuring her words carefully. After a few moments, she said, "Probably."

He clapped his hands together and grinned. "Good. Give me a couple of minutes to call the ranch and we can get started."

She stayed put on the tractor while he called his dad; reinforcements would be over within the hour. Depending on how many guys were free, it might be possible to get all the trees in the ground this afternoon. A mechanical planter was something she didn't own since established orchards didn't replant trees every year, so he had asked Joe to get the fence post auger ready.

He opened the cooler and withdrew two bottles of water and the container of cookies. He wasn't above using baked goods as a way to sweeten her up, and he happened to know she was partial to any cookie his mom made.

He sauntered over to her and she caught the bottle he tossed to her with ease, and then he gently shook the plastic container. "Cookie?"

Her eyes brightened. "Your mom's?"

"Of course." He stepped onto the narrow running board and settled on the fender. "Where do you want to start?" He looked over his shoulder at the neatly stacked pallets on the wagon. "Did you load all of these today?"

With a lighthearted chuckle, she said, "I'm not Wonder Woman." She snagged a cookie and Hank couldn't help himself; he took two.

She rolled her eyes while she groaned with pleasure as she took the first bite. Once upon a time she used to—well, he wasn't going to dwell on the pleasure she'd taken when he'd kissed her.

With a grin, she said, "I had the truck driver unload directly onto the wagon; it saved me a lot of work this morning."

"Always thinking, just like when we were younger."

"Speaking of." She flipped the key and the engine sputtered to a low grumble. "Let's start unloading the stock in the furthest spot and work our way forward, then we can go back to the barn and load up again."

"If we time it right, the guys might be here to help." He unbuttoned his shirt pocket and pulled out his cell phone. "I'll let them know to meet us at the barn."

She held up her hands, palm side up. "Whatever." She leaned in and brushed her lips to his cheek in a featherlight kiss. "I'm done protesting, so thank you."

His heart skipped a beat with the brush of her lips on his cheek. If he kissed her, he wondered if he could make her sigh too. But he reminded himself to keep this friendly and not overcomplicate things between them—or worse, start something he couldn't finish.

He held up a finger. "Hey, Dad, can you let the guys know to meet us at the barn? We'll need to load up the trailer and get the trees out to the field."

He listened. "Sure thing, and let Joe know we need a couple of trailers too; we could get all the stock out to the field in one shot."

Efficiency was his dad's middle name and it wouldn't surprise him if his dad had everything running like a well-oiled gear in ten minutes. He was about to hang up when his dad said, "Hold on a minute; Mom wants to talk to you."

"Hank, it's Mom."

He grinned. It was so like his mother to make an announcement for something he already knew, but she was the sweetest woman so what did it matter? "Hey, Mom."

"Would you ask Renee if she'd like to come for dinner

tonight? And before you do, I won't take no for an answer. After working all day, she'll probably eat a bowl of cereal standing next to the sink and she needs a decent meal."

"I'll ask her but I'm not guaranteeing anything."

She cocked a brow and mouthed, *What?*

He held up his index finger.

"Son, remind her that I've driven over to pick her up before when she turned me down and tonight could be a repeat performance."

"Yes, ma'am. I'll give her the message." He stuck the phone in his shirt pocket. "Mom said you *must* come for dinner and if you refuse, she's driving over to pick you up."

"Ah, she's pulling that trick." She smiled. "When I was a sophomore in college and my parents went on vacation, she asked me to come for dinner and when I said maybe and then didn't show up, she was knocking on my door at six o'clock on the dot. Your mom got it into her head I was gonna wither away and starve before my parents returned and they were only gone for a long weekend." A slow smile appeared as she slipped down memory lane. "Dinner sounds good."

At a loss by her quick agreement, he said, "We should unload; otherwise, the men will be here and we won't be ready."

She dropped the tractor in gear and he kept an eye on her from the corner of his. If it was possible, she was even more beautiful, and he felt that old familiar tug. He had to keep denying the way his heart beat faster wasn't just because he was near her. After all, he had spent his entire adult life lying to himself. Time hadn't changed his heart.

*R*enee grabbed the iron rake from the wheelbarrow and smoothed out the dirt around the base of the tree. She looked around. They were more than half done and it was going faster than she'd dreamed. The Stone's Throw Ranch hands worked harder than anyone she had hired. It wasn't because there was anything extra in this for them, and then it dawned on her. The people she hired were on the clock; if they took their time, they got paid more.

She kicked a clod of dirt in Hank's direction and he straightened up, but the cowboy hat obscured his eyes.

He asked, "Got a burr under your saddle?"

She cut the next sapling out of its protective burlap cover and pulled the roots from the ball. "Nothing." She focused on the ground in front of her, doing her best to mask her annoyance. There was no sense seeing if he could still figure out what she was thinking at almost any given moment. It had always been that way between the two of them; with one look and a simple question, there would be no secrets between them and she needed to keep a few—mainly the big one. She finally faced the truth; she never stopped loving him. It hadn't been an immature love they had tossed away; it had been the real deal.

She looked again at the ranch hands and back to the hole she was placing the tree into.

"So, it's like that?" His voice was as smooth as honey.

She lifted her eyes to meet his. "What are you talking about?"

"Either you're unhappy with the job we're doing or you're unhappy with the previous crew."

She clenched her hands around the shovel and proceeded to widen the hole. "Just stop doing that."

"Working?"

She wiggled her index finger at him. "In addition to planting trees, your brain is pitching like a bucking stallion at the rodeo."

He lifted a shoulder and dropped it. "I can't help it if I'm concerned about you."

His words drifted off and she could barely hear what he said next. "Hank, if you have something to say, speak up."

He was just poking at her so she'd fess up, but it wasn't going to work.

Not this time.

His words came out crystal clear. "I said it's too bad you didn't have decent help, not just to get the trees planted but to install the fence too."

The last thing she needed to be reminded about was the stupid fence. It had been a calculated risk, but this had been the first time a bunch of dumb cows wandered across the river. How was she supposed to know they found a section of fence down?

"There are only so many hours in a day." The shovel bit into the softened earth and she silently thanked her lucky stars for that; the planting was going smoothly.

He crossed to the wagon and grabbed two more trees

before setting them on the ground and leaned against the side. "I'll make a deal with you."

Past experience reminded her that Hank never made a deal he didn't intend on winning. But curiosity would get the best of her in the long run so it was better just to ask and save them both some time. "I'll bite."

He pushed the brim of his cowboy hat back with his finger, like a gunslinger in an old spaghetti Western. A glint lit up his eyes. If it were one hundred years in the past, she'd guess his fingers would be flexing, getting ready to draw if the deal wasn't agreed to. But he wasn't wearing a six-gun on his hip and Hank would never hurt any living creature.

"If my men get the trees planted today, we'll come back tomorrow and get that fence of yours installed."

She cocked her head and narrowed her eyes. "What's in it for you?" What could he possibly have up his sleeve?

"If we pull off both of these jobs, not only will you have dinner at my parents' tonight, but tomorrow night we'll go out for dinner and pie at Maggie's diner."

Somehow it sounded almost too good to be true. Not only would her trees get planted, but she'd have a fence and two good dinners she didn't have to cook.

"Sounds like you'll be getting the short end of the straw." But it would give her an excellent excuse to see him two more times before he left town. Since she had bumped into Hank at the hospital and was now spending time with him, things had changed. *Should I go all into this relationship or be like the Tin Man, wanting love but not having it?* She squinted her eyes and studied his face. *But I love him. If I don't take the risk I definitely won't have it.* Her fingertips itched to run along his angled jaw. Curling them into the palm of her hand she pushed that visual aside. *What the heck. Wasn't it better to have loved and lost than never to have loved at all?*

She thrust out her hand and gave his a firm shake. Before she released it, she squeezed. "Just so we're clear, your guys have to finish the trees today and get the fence up tomorrow, right?"

"That's right."

She was almost a little disappointed. There was no way they'd get all the fencing done in one day, not with the six of them working from dawn till dusk, and the ranch hands had other responsibilities too.

A grin blossomed across his face and he held her hand a little longer than necessary. "Just remember, you put zero conditions on this deal."

Her radar pinged like a bat at night. Hank was up to something and by the smirk on his face, she thought she'd just made a deal with a handsome devil. "Trees and fencing. Not much else to say."

He let out an ear-piercing whistle and his guys looked up. He waved his arm overhead like he was using a lasso on an errant cow. But in this instance, it was telling them to speed things up. He got a thumbs-up from one of the men. Then he withdrew his cell and punched in a few numbers.

"Dad, we need more men over here. We've got fencing to install and we'll need all the equipment to go with it." He listened and grinned. "And can you ask Mom to make up her award-winning chocolate cake for dessert?" He nodded. "Yeah, that's the one, Renee's favorite." He gave her a saucy wink and her heart skipped a couple of beats.

She knew she'd walked right into that deal with her eyes wide open.

Not that it mattered. She was going to extract every bit of fun she could from the next couple of days.

He returned his cell to his jeans pocket. "And that's how a deal is won."

"All right, smart aleck. You may have set things in

motion, but the trees aren't in yet and there's a lot of fencing to be installed."

"Darlin', if there's one thing you should never forget when it comes to me, I always finish what I start. All that's left to decide is what time I'm picking you up tomorrow night."

She loved his confidence and he was right about one thing. Hank Shepard always found a way to make things happen—and on his schedule too.

"Seven o'clock would be just fine."

He waved a hand in front of her. "Six. We want to make sure we have plenty of time to linger over dinner and dessert and if you play your cards right, I might just take you out for a little stargazing too."

"Cocky." She grinned and walked away but not before she said over her shoulder, "Stargazing is on the table if *you* play your cards right."

He laughed loud and long as she continued to plant trees; after all, two dates were riding on getting this job done on time.

*H*ank had picked her up at exactly six. Dinner with Henry and Maeve was delicious as always and she'd had fun. Now that they were in Hank's truck, she rested a plate, covered with foil, in her lap that had two thick slices of the chocolate cake Maeve had insisted she take. It'd be delicious with her morning coffee, but after she ate something like eggs to counterbalance all the sugar and butter. From the corner of her eye, she stole a look at Hank's angular profile.

"Thanks for tonight. I had a good time and I'm glad your mom insisted that I come."

"They loved seeing you. I didn't realize you all have standing monthly dinner plans."

Hank navigated the truck over a well-worn dirt road on their way to the overlook, their special place. Driving out there tonight had been her idea and Hank was quick to agree; it held many sweet memories for them. They had spent countless nights stargazing and more when they were in high school. It had been where they shared their first and last kiss. It was also the place where they made the decision to go to different colleges.

She gazed out the window and thought how naïve they had been. "Do you ever think about that night?"

In this case, she was glad explanations weren't necessary. He'd know what night she referred to.

"All the time." He gave her hand a squeeze and she absorbed his warmth like she'd been brought in from a Montana winter and set in front of a roaring fire.

"Do you have regrets?" His voice was soft, and the slow, steady tenor of his voice matched the beat of her heart.

"Regrets aren't how I live my life. I look forward but I learn from the past."

He slowed as they approached the old grove of ponderosa pines. Once parked, he released his seat belt and turned toward her. "There are times where I wish we had a do-over. If I could go back to the younger me, I'd tell myself to find a way to keep in touch, do the work to stay friends."

"But we had to follow our dreams." That was how she had thought about the past too. If only.

"We did, but friendship would have kept us connected. I've missed your honesty and way of looking at life. You never let me skate by when things got tough; you challenged me to reach for the stars."

"Did you touch any?" She swallowed the lump in her throat. Being here with him tonight was harder than she thought it would be.

"I did but it was a small victory without you telling me to stretch beyond, to keep pushing and find new goals."

His voice was thick with emotion. Being with Hank tonight was as if no time had passed between them. She knew in her heart by the way he looked at her and touched her hand he felt it too.

"And now?" Did she dare hope that he would say something to lead them down the road to a new future?

"I came back to help out Dad and I never expected to run into you, much less spend time with you before I went home."

She withdrew her hand.

"The more time we spend together, the more confused I get." His finger traced along her jawline and he tipped her chin up before lowering his lips to hers. It was a gentle, tender kiss with raw emotion bubbling under the surface.

She wanted to keep kissing him but that wasn't the right thing to do. He was leaving; Dallas was his home now just as her home was Montana. The tentative hope of what she had dared to dream—of a new romance—was crushed. She had to keep reminding herself of this hard truth. Renee turned her face to her window. "Will you take me home now, please?"

12

*H*ank went slack-jawed. The last thing he had expected was for Renee to ask him to take her home. He'd hoped to stay out here all night like they used to do, talking about their hopes and dreams for the future, just being together. But her words were like being doused with ice water.

"Of course." They drove back to the farm in silence, only the sound of the engine for company. Renee had withdrawn into herself. But they still had tomorrow working on the fence together, and then she had promised him dinner out. Would it be right to hold her to the promise? Even if he wanted to, he'd never pressure her into going; everything was in her hands. He glanced her way and the sad expression on her face gutted him. What had he done to cause her so much pain? As he replayed their conversation, nothing came to mind. They had been enjoying their time together and once they started talking about reaching for the stars, he should have said his life was hollow without her by his side. *But how can I admit that to her? She'll think less of me, won't she?*

He pulled up next to the side porch of the farmhouse

and turned off the truck. Before she could get out, he said, "Please wait a moment."

He hurried around to the passenger side and opened the door for her, holding out his hand. Her fingers grazed his, sending his heart into a stampede. He walked her to the door and stood under the same porch light he had a thousand times before.

"Renee, I don't know what I said that made you sad, but I'm sorry. I wanted tonight to be enjoyable for both of us."

"You didn't do anything; it's just the way our lives turned out. I do care about you but we're on different paths. Soon you'll be headed back to Dallas and I'll be growing apples. We're both where we want to be, and it wouldn't do any good to pretend otherwise. To pretend that we might have more would be to set us both up for more heartache." She said, "Thank you for taking me to your parents' place and for the drive." She stood on tiptoes and brushed her lips over his cheek.

Her soft floral scent teased his senses. It was another sucker punch to the gut, a reminder of what once was.

She stepped back and opened the door. Then she looked at him as if memorizing his face. "I'll understand if you don't want to come around tomorrow to help with the fence. I'll take care of it."

He tipped his head. "And if I want to?"

Her face softened into a small smile. "I've learned to never refuse an act of genuine kindness. In case I haven't said it, thank you for everything you've done to help me. It means more than you know."

"You're welcome. Now... what about the second half of our bargain?" His heart thumped in his chest and his mouth went dry. He hoped she'd say they were still on for dinner at Maggie's.

She gave him a long look, as if she might be weighing the pros and cons of continuing with their deal. "The fence isn't finished yet so no telling if we'll be going out tomorrow night."

His heart soared; she wasn't saying no. "No worries, that fence will be up and secured before dinnertime."

Her laugh caressed his ears. It was a sound he could hear for the rest of his life. Before he could think of anything witty to say, she wished him a good night, held up the cake plate and said thank you again, before she softly closed the door, leaving him standing under the porch light alone.

He strolled back to his truck and glanced over his shoulder. He could see her progress as she flicked on lights in each room. She had never been a fan of the dark and in a small way it was nice to see that some things hadn't changed.

Tomorrow when we have dinner, I'll see what I can do to keep that sweet smile on her face. He dropped the truck in gear. Before he went home, he'd swing by the bunkhouse to make sure all hands were ready to work at light speed. He even reached out to his old friend,—Lincoln Cooper, at the Grace Star Ranch—for extra hands to get the job finished. He knew how to make things happen and he wasn't about to take any chances on blowing his date with Renee.

*T*he next morning Hank hopped in his truck for the short ride over to Renee's place. On his way down the drive, he noticed a bunch of guys standing around pickup trucks loaded with tools and there was a post hole digger attached to a tractor. Now they'd have three, one they had left at the orchard yesterday and another from Linc Cooper. He lifted his hand and smiled. Everyone was pulling together and all that was left to do was get started. Renee was going to be surprised when she saw how many people had come to pitch in.

Hank turned into Renee's driveway and the tires kicked up dust and gravel. He swung by her house but figured she was already in the orchard since her tractor was gone, but a late model SUV was parked near the house and it had Illinois plates. Curiosity piqued, he wondered if Ginny was back.

He slowed as he approached the area they had planted yesterday and there she was, unhooking a flatbed wagon filled with fence posts. His admiration for her grew. She might be getting help today, but she wasn't one to sit by and let people do the work for her. Looking around, he saw she was alone. Maybe that wasn't Ginny's vehicle.

Once the truck was parked near the tree line, he waved. "Renee." He hoped to get her attention. He didn't want to walk up and potentially scare her. She had a hair-trigger sense of fight-or-flight and from this distance he could see the woman was holding wire clippers in her hand. "Renee," he shouted again as he got closer. She was totally focused on what she was working on.

Finally, she looked up and shielded her eyes with the back of her hand. "Hank, what are you doing here already?"

He held up his arm where his watch normally rested. "As a rancher, former or present, we get up early to start our day. The cattle don't sleep in."

She tossed the cutters to the edge of the wagon. "I didn't expect you so early. I thought I'd get a jump on things." She looked over his shoulder. "Are you by yourself?"

"A couple of guys will be along soon. They were loading up when I left. Hey, whose SUV is at the house?"

"Ginny. She got in around one so I expect we'll see her later." A grin twitched her lips. "Now about this project. Looks like no dinner for us tonight."

He jammed his hands in his Levi's. "Is that hope or disappointment in your voice?"

"Well, you just said"—she did air quotes—"a couple of guys are headed this way, but you and I both know it's gonna take a small but mighty army of people to get this fence up and around the acreage."

"We're talking around four thousand feet of fence. Not to worry, we'll be done by sundown."

She snorted a laugh and shook her head. "You're awfully confident, Shepard. Care to make the bet double or nothing?"

He gave her a side-eye look. "Huh, how about we agree that if the fence is finished, not only will you have dinner in town with me tonight, but we'll take a picnic down to the river over the weekend."

"Do I have to pack said picnic basket?" She pressed her lips together trying to keep the grin from growing.

"Nope."

She tapped her chin. "But at the moment this little bargain only gives you what you want. How about if you don't succeed? What do I get?"

"I think our arrangement suits us both but go ahead if you want to sweeten your side of the agreement. Tell me what you'd like." He leaned against the side of the wagon, wishing she'd spill it. All too soon the jig would be up, and she'd know that the army she thought didn't exist would be pulling in.

"I can't think of anything under all this pressure, so if the fence isn't finished, I can tweak the bargain and you'll have to agree." She stuck out her hand. "What do you say?"

He could see the sparkle in her eyes, and this was a no-brainer. He'd always do whatever she wanted, but by the end of today, her new trees would be planted and protected and he'd have two dates with this lovely woman standing in front of him. He clasped her hand with his and then covered the top of her hand with his other one.

"I can't wait to see your face when we drive the last

fence post and secure the last section." He gave her a wink. "And if I might suggest, wear something blue tonight—it makes your eyes pop."

A low rumble from the road drew her attention. Clouds of dust camouflaged the army that had arrived. Her eyes widened. "Hank, how many favors did you have to call in?"

Two tractors with augers and pickup trucks with flatbed trailers were right behind them.

"No favors. I just asked good friends to lend a hand." He brushed back a lock of hair from her cheek. "They're your friends too, Renee."

Her mouth hung open and she was speechless for several long moments. She brushed away the tears that appeared on her lashes and murmured, "Thank you."

He pulled his leather gloves from his back pocket. He hadn't wanted to make her cry, even if they were tears of joy. "Come on, Sunshine. It's fencing time."

*H*ank noticed when his mom parked her SUV near a wagon that his dad was riding shotgun. She set out baskets of food on the flatbed trailer and as usual she had more than enough for everyone. Fencing days were draining and she had witnessed many in her years on the ranch. His dad waved from the chair his mom had set up for him and Hank jogged over to him.

"Hey, Dad, how's it looking?"

"Real good. Do I see Linc Cooper over there?"

"You do and he brought nine of his men so altogether, we're running a crew of twenty-two including me and Renee."

"Good thing your mom packed the entire kitchen to feed everyone." He gave Hank a wide smile. "A nice thing you're doing here."

"I'd do anything for her." He turned and watched as she pulled a roll of metal fence wire from the back of another wagon. She had shown everyone right from the start she could hold her own.

"Except move back to Montana?"

Hank was taken aback by his dad's question. "Why. Do you think she would welcome me back?"

"Some things haven't changed. I saw the way she looked at you last night. There aren't many times in life you get a second chance with the woman you've always loved. In case you haven't noticed, she's unattached and so are you."

"We've been over this. I work in Texas."

"Since I paid for that education, I happen to know you passed the bar in two states. The only thing that's preventing you from moving home is you. Did you forget Robert Adler is retiring? He has a thriving business, and I'm sure you could take over his practice."

His mom made her way over to them. "You've got your serious faces on. What are you talking about?"

Hank glanced at his father. "Mending fences."

"And building them," his dad said.

He knew exactly what his father wanted to hear and now was not the time to discuss his love life, least of all with his parents. He dropped a kiss on the top of his mom's head.

"Thanks for bringing lunch over. I won't be home for dinner."

"A date with someone we know?" His mom's eyes twinkled and there was a hopeful note in her voice. She had never made it a secret she'd welcome a reconciliation between Renee and Hank. "Perhaps the pea to your pod?"

"Dinner with a very good friend." He nodded to the people working. "I need to get back to work but thanks again for feeding everyone and I'll bring the baskets home."

His dad cautiously rose to his feet, leaning heavily on his cane. Mom took his other arm as they moved in the direction of the SUV.

Hank said, "Watch out for the potholes on your way out."

His dad gave him a wink. "You've got time for another project before you leave. I'm stepping back into the day-to-day workings of our ranch when my sick leave is over next week."

"Dad, did you just fire me?" He wanted to laugh but his father had an ulterior motive that was as clear as a pane of glass.

"Someone needs to take action and if you're not willing, I can."

Hank watched as his parents drove in a zigzag pattern down the gravel road. That was something he could fix.

13

*R*enee collapsed on the old floral sofa and eased her sock-clad feet onto the coffee table as she let out an audible groan. Ginny handed her a glass filled with ice and seltzer.

"Tough day?"

After a sip of the refreshing drink, Renee said, "I've never worked so hard in all my life and for the record, I'm not in any kind of shape to have a repeat day anytime soon."

Ginny tossed her another pillow from the chair. "For your feet."

She smiled her thanks and propped them up with a hope it would ease the throbbing in her arches.

"I'm sorry I didn't get out there to work but I overslept. Then my publisher called and that conversation took forever."

With a dismissive wave of her hand, Renee said, "No worries. As you saw, Hank had most of River Junction working in my field today. I still can't believe the fence is finished and all the trees are planted. I had my doubts, but he made it happen."

She wiggled her eyebrows. "From where I sit, he had incentive."

"What, the two dinner dates?" She shook her head. "More like it eases his guilt over what his father's cattle did. I won't go reading too much into it."

"I don't know about that. Maybe you're not reading enough into it. What time is he picking you up?"

"Originally it was six but the way my body feels, like it was run over by the tractor, I suggested seven. I need a long, hot shower and time to get ready."

Renee finished her seltzer and set the glass on the pine table next to her. She arched a brow. "There were some good-looking cowboys working hard out there today. Any catch your eye? If you describe them, I might be able to wrangle an introduction."

"I hadn't noticed. Besides, I read in a book when an engagement ends to give yourself plenty of time before you start dating again. The last thing I need is a rebound romance."

With a roll of her eyes, Renee said, "That might be the best way to get over the jerk who shall remain nameless."

Ginny gave her a sad smile. "I appreciate your support and even offering to set me up. Until I know what I want, I'm going to work on me and cheer on your romantic endeavors from the sidelines."

"Of which there are zero real prospects. I know for a fact Hank is looking forward to getting back to Dallas." Her chin rested on her chest. "He called it home."

Ginny crossed the room and the sofa dipped as she sat down next to Renee. "That doesn't mean his old feelings haven't resurfaced. Right before you left Chicago, you said there was no chance in hell those embers existed. Now look. Flash forward six months and they're not just embers. I saw that twinkle in your eye when you were talking to him today. Dang, girl, the fire is established and hot enough to roast a marshmallow."

She gave a snort. "That's quite an image. As long as Hank is the marshmallow."

Ginny took Renee's hand and turned it palm side up. "Do you see those blisters that are hovering beneath the surface?"

"Not only can I see them, but they sting too. Where are you going with this?"

"By the time I got to the field, the fencing was almost complete and I noticed that you kept pace with Hank, shovel for shovel. But you weren't grumbling about how hard it was to keep going. You were never like that with anyone you dated before."

"He makes working fun—but enough talk of Hank." She pushed herself to a more upright position. "I want to hear all about your meeting and what's the status with your new book?"

Ginny's face drooped. "I'm behind in perfecting the recipes and writing the copy. The publisher is itching to schedule the photo shoot, but that can't happen until I've finalized what recipes are going in the book."

"What's holding you back?" Renee was ready to do whatever was needed to support her friend.

"Me. It's not like I'm depressed, but my creative mojo is lacking. I don't have the drive to measure out a bunch of ingredients. I'd rather help you plant trees."

"That, my friend, is called procrastination. And the good news is, since all the trees are planted until the next shipment, you have plenty of time to cook." She gingerly stood up and waited for her muscles to stop protesting before she moved. "In fact, my day tomorrow is light. How about I be your dishwasher and official taste tester. You stopped at the market when you were in Bozeman, right?"

"Yeah, but—"

Renee narrowed her eyes and gave her friend a steady look. "No buts. While I'm out, make a list of what you'd like to accomplish tomorrow, from just enough to beyond your wildest expectations and we'll finish somewhere in the middle." She pointed to the stairs. "Now I'm going to climb those stairs with what little energy I have left and stand under a hot shower until the water runs cold." With slow hobble, she crossed the living room. She placed a firm grip on the banister and made her way up, one stair at a time.

"I'll bring you a big mug of ginger tea and honey. It will help with the soreness you're feeling and give you a shot of energy so you don't fall asleep in your soup."

Renee paused mid-step. "I might need more than tea to stay awake until dinner but at least it's an idea." She finished climbing the stairs, wishing she could cancel dinner with Hank. Not because of him but she was beyond exhausted and there was a grain of truth in what Ginny said: she might fall asleep during dinner if there was any lull in the conversation and that would be embarrassing.

*G*inny knocked on her bedroom door and eased it open. "Can I come in?"

Renee was pushing a hanger aside as she rifled through her closet. "Sure."

She held out a mug and Renee took it and sipped. There was enough honey for a beehive and it tasted like ambrosia. "Thanks for this."

"You're welcome. Did the shower help?"

"As fixes go, it was great, but tomorrow I won't be setting any speed records. I just pushed the ache deeper into the muscles. Oh, and I took a couple of Tylenol too." She waved the mug at the pair of black jeans on the bed.

"I'm in search of a blue top to go with these pants; they're a slim-fit so I need something to cover part of my backside."

"With your curves, girl, flaunt them. You've got a figure that I envy so don't hide it under some oversized top." She waved Renee aside. "Allow me to be your stylist for the evening." With a roll of one shoulder and a wink, she said, "I'll make sure to pick out casual but with enough sass it will cause Mr. Shepard to rethink his comment about leaving."

Unwilling to argue her choice in clothes or that Hank was leaving soon, Renee sat down at her desk and concentrated on the warm mug clasped in her hands. With each sip, she started to perk up. Maybe the pain reliever and the tea were kicking in. "I was thinking about what you said earlier. When you said we work well together." The *we* was her and Hank and it felt natural to couple them up into a "we" again. She had expected exhaustion to overwhelm her after the day she put in working side by side with him. Instead, she was pleasantly surprised to realize she was exhilarated at seeing him again.

"And you kind of left me hanging with that statement. But never mind." Ginny didn't turn around but continued to pull blouses from the closet and then return them. "I do know we're going shopping for some decent date clothes. Everything in here is either super casual or office wear. Did you donate your entire dating wardrobe?"

She snorted. "I never had a dating wardrobe. Dinner and a movie never needed high fashion and it still doesn't."

Ginny frowned at her. "Pretty clothes are for us, not for the men in our lives."

"Well, I don't have a man, exactly. I am having dinner with an old friend who won a bet that I should have given more thought to before I agreed."

"Aha!" Ginny pulled out a silky sapphire-blue blouse and held it up. "This is what you're going to wear."

"I don't know. It's a bit clingy." She drained the last of the tea and put the mug on the desk. "There has to be something less fancy in there. What about a turtleneck sweater?"

"Stop. This is a basic blue shirt with buttons." She wiggled the hanger and the shirt shimmered in the lamplight. "It'll look great with those black jeans, a pair of booties, and the leather blazer I saw in the back of the closet." She tossed the shirt from across the room, and Renee caught it. "Just try it on and if you really hate it, I'll find something else. But trust me, with your flawless complexion and auburn hair, this shirt completes the perfect outfit."

With a grin, Ginny pointed to the door. "I'll see you downstairs and don't forget a spritz of perfume behind your ears, just in case the handsome cowboy-turned-lawyer wants to get a little closer."

Renee pointed to the door. "Out." She wasn't upset with Ginny, but the more she talked, the more nervous Renee became. To have an expectation that tonight could lead to other nights caused her stomach to flip. *We're still in the friend zone, even if I want something more. Unless he makes his feelings clear, I needed to be careful, so my heart will be intact once he leaves.*

With her new approach to life—and Hank—in place, Renee held the blouse up in front of her and looked in the mirror. Ginny had been right; the color was perfect, but she'd need a great pair of earrings and knew just what to wear.

As she descended the stairs, she heard Hank's voice. He was a couple of minutes early, just like always, and she smiled. *Some things never change.* When she entered the living room, Ginny gave her a thumbs-up, slipped into the den, and closed the door.

The smile on Hank's lips warmed his eyes and assured her he was looking forward to tonight as much as she was.

He crossed the room, took her hand, and brushed his lips to her cheek. "You look great." He lingered close and said, "Love the perfume."

Renee dipped her head, hoping to hide her cheeks which she knew would get deep pink from the compliment. Looking at his black boots, jeans, and creamy white shirt with a dark-gray blazer, she said, "You're looking handsome tonight too."

"Thank you." From behind his back, he withdrew a bouquet of bright-yellow flowers with a light-brown center.

She squeezed her eyes shut to push away the pinpricks of tears. He remembered she loved arrowleaf balsamroot, an early flower that grew around here but not on her land. He must have found a patch on the way over.

"For you."

"Thank you." She took them and went into the kitchen; they needed to be put in water. She grabbed a glass pitcher she normally made tea in, which would be the perfect substitute for a vase. It really was sweet of him, and she looked at him from under her lashes. Did he remember or was it just a lucky guess?

"Are they still your favorites?" Tall with wide shoulders, he filled the doorway. Her heart skipped again. *I need to get my feelings under control before I have an angina attack.* She smiled at the thought. He had already zapped her heart; it was hammering in her chest right now and it was good to feel the blood pulsing in her veins. "Yes, they are. It was sweet you remembered."

"There's very little I forget and that includes simple pleasures like flowers and"—he pulled a chocolate bar from his shirt pocket and handed it to her—"dark chocolate with coconut."

If things were different, she would have thrown her

arms around his neck and kissed him senseless. The gesture was thoughtful and he was right; simple things did mean the most.

She crooked her finger and he came closer. Throwing caution to the wind, she brushed her lips over his. She drank in his woodsy cologne and on his breath, she could smell the lingering aroma of the same sweet treat he had just given her. She swatted his arm as she stepped back. "You had one?"

He laughed and slipped his arms around her waist, pulling her close to his chest. "Quality control purposes only." He lowered his mouth to hers but stopped when there was a wisp of air between them, waiting for her to make the next move.

She tipped her head to the side and gave him a slow, sweet kiss. But as her thoughts began to cloud her better judgment, she stepped back and looked at the floor. She didn't want him to see the love she knew would be in her eyes. In the last three days, she had not only cracked the protective shell over her heart but tossed it on the garbage pile. But she wasn't ready to throw caution to the wind.

"I don't know about you, but I've worked up quite the appetite. I wonder what Maggie's got for specials tonight."

He took half a step back as if he understood her withdrawal and respected it. "Don't forget to save room for pie too."

"I might even bring a slice home." She slung her bag across her body and took the house keys from the table. "I'm ready."

14

*H*ank pushed open the kitchen door and let Renee walk ahead of him. The sun wasn't ready to call it a day for another hour. He remembered she loved late April as the days grew longer and the nights were still cool. He held the passenger door for her, then went around to his side. He waited for a moment to steady his racing heart and then got in.

At the end of the driveway, he turned onto the main road which led into town.

Renee asked, "Have you been to the diner since you've been back?"

"No, I've been busy with the ranch and since Dad's been home, Mom's been making all his favorite meals. Which happen to be mine too so there hasn't been a need to go into town."

"Getting your fill of home cooking is never a bad idea, especially when your mom's in front of the stove."

"She's pretty talented but so is your mom; her brownies are amazing. Will your parents come back this summer?"

"That's the plan. I think late June."

He thought, with Ginny staying a while, it must break up the quiet but he didn't say that to her.

"I'm looking forward to them coming home. I plan on picking Dad's brain about the darn cider press too. Tony's been trying to fix it but we still can't get it working smoothly. If I want to grow the business, a better understanding of why he made the decisions he did could prove to be invaluable."

"Gaining insight on the business is always valuable but I'm sorry I'll miss them." And there it was, a sharp reminder their time together was fleeting. But that wasn't something he needed to dwell on.

"I'll give them your best." Her voice cracked as they turned down Main Street, past the bank, movie theater, and hardware store before he pulled up in front of the diner. From outside he could see it was bustling with midweek activity which meant tables would be at a premium and they might have to wait.

They walked inside and Maggie's smile welcomed them. "Hey, you two. I wondered when you'd find your way in for dinner." She pointed to a booth near the back. "Take a seat and I'll be right over."

Hank looked around. Not much had changed with the black-and-white floor tiles and booths along the front windows with their bright-blue vinyl cushions. Full tables were packed in close, and there wasn't an open stool at the counter. Mack, the cook, who was older than dirt, was still putting out mouthwatering meals at a rapid pace based on what he could see. He'd been there for as long as anyone could remember and there was nobody who could make pancakes like him.

Hank let Renee choose which bench seat she wanted but for a change she didn't face the restaurant to watch the comings and goings of people; she focused on Hank.

He tapped the paper in front of her and gave a snort.

"Look at this. The basic menu is still printed on the placemats."

"The best things never change, Hank."

He wanted to say, "Look at how I feel about you; that didn't change even though I tried to forget." Instead, he pretended to study the menu.

Maggie handed them a paper with the dinner specials and then left them to decide.

Renee placed her hand on top of the menu. "Hey, I have a great idea. Do you want to share two different meals?"

He looked up and grinned. "What are you thinking?"

"The chicken fried steak and fried chicken with dumplings. We're celebrating the completion of two major projects." She pointed to the drink list. "But I'll skip the milkshake in favor of pie after. My metabolism isn't what it was when we were teenagers."

"Truth. I'll have to hit the gym regularly when I'm back home. I've gotten used to eating more."

A frown graced her face as he referred to Dallas.

"You don't need a gym out here."

He passed her a paper napkin. "I've forgotten all the different muscles you use when working on a ranch. I'll admit I had a few days of aches and pains. But it's all good now."

After they gave Maggie their order, an uncomfortable silence settled over them. Hank fiddled with his fork and napkin, stabbing little holes into the paper. "Tell me about Chicago. Did you like living there?"

"That seems like a lifetime ago now. I've been home since the fall and not once have I thought about going back to the insanity of traffic and the congestion of people. It was something I hadn't recognized until my inner spring unwound once I dug into work at the orchard. I'm busy but it's a different kind of pace."

"Were you happy there and did you enjoy your job

designing office spaces for corporations? They always feel sterile and it's too bad since many people spend a lot of time at the office."

"Exactly. I wanted people to feel good, like it was a home away from home if that makes any sense."

He looked her straight in the eye. "And did you find someone special?"

She met his gaze and didn't blink. "I dated but never found that special connection with any guy I met."

He wanted to ask if that's how she had felt being with him, here and now.

"What about you? Does big city life trip your trigger? What am I saying? It must or you wouldn't be looking forward to going back."

He knew exactly what she was saying. Talking about Dallas as a statement of fact kept him grounded, reiterating there was no future here. He didn't want to fall into the chasm of loving Renee again. "I like my job at the law firm; it keeps me on my toes, but there isn't much time for fun."

"There's no one special waiting for you?"

Did she really want to know or was this part of polite conversation? "Nope. Like you, I've never made that special connection with anyone, besides you." Why had he acknowledged the connection he knew they still shared?

She looked at him, her breath shallow. "What, you're not involved?"

He reached across the off-white Formica table and waited for her to take his hand. She placed hers in his and warmth spread through him.

"Renee, you're impossible to forget." He gave her hand a squeeze. "And I'm hoping I might be unforgettable too."

He knew her favorite song was by Nat King Cole and now he linked that to this conversation. Could she be bold and speak the undeniable truth or would putting her heart on the line make her feel like a fool? Heck, he understood she was taking chances in every aspect of her life, leaving a lucrative career to be a farmer, and that was a career path that wasn't for the faint of heart.

"I still love you, but I'm not expecting anything from you."

Stunned didn't begin to describe how he felt the moment Renee said she was still in love with him. But in the next breath, she seemed to dismiss those feelings too.

He wished there wasn't a table between them or that they weren't in a public place. He'd take her in his arms and show her just how much he loved her. Her face dropped and she balled the paper napkin in her hand. Was sharing her innermost feelings unbearable for her?

Taking the napkin from her, Hank set it aside and dipped his head so that he could make eye contact. "That was the sweetest thing you've ever said to me."

She let a small smile grace her kissable lips. "I wanted to tell you how I feel, no matter what may come of our time together."

So that was it, the reason she had pulled back. The end of this moment in time. She recognized it but he got a glimmer of hope. Could they do something long distance? Although the miles between here and Dallas seemed endless, he could make a point of coming home more often. He certainly had enough paid time off banked, and they could video chat and text. It was possible if they really wanted to stay connected.

He caressed her cheek with his thumb. "We live in the twenty-first century and there's amazing technology so we can stay in touch—text, email, video calls, and airplanes."

"This isn't something we need to talk about tonight, Hank. We should enjoy our dinner and make plans for the picnic we're going on this weekend. Those are things we should be focused on, not trying to figure out if or how to keep in touch when you leave." She leaned against the vinyl cushion and tucked her hands in her lap.

He understood it was easier when they weren't touching, he felt the same. But he wanted to be close with her, and every time they seemed to take a step in that direction, one of them pulled back.

Maggie delivered their dinners along with two extra plates for sharing. "Enjoy." She bustled away to the next table, leaving them alone in the busy diner.

After they passed half of their meals to the other, Hank sliced off a piece of chicken fried steak. As he savored the unique flavor, he thought about how they seemed to be tap-dancing around the topic of the past.

"Renee." He put his fork down. "I think we need to clear the air about what happened all those years ago."

Her eyes grew wide and she shook her head. "There's nothing to rehash. We were young and had strong feelings for each other, but as kids we didn't know how to make a long-distance relationship work."

He nodded in agreement but there was more to it than that. He was hurt she didn't pick up and follow him.

"We had different life goals. If I had just trotted along behind you, going to the college you attended just so we could be together, what did that say about me? I needed to find my own way in the world. Being an interior designer was important to me just as going into law was your dream. Like Robert Frost said, there were two roads in the wood; I happened to take the road that was best suited for me and you took the other."

"It would have been nice to go to college together."

She stopped cutting the chicken and gave him a long look. He knew what that meant; she was measuring her words carefully.

"If I had asked you to go to college in Chicago instead of New York, would you have followed me?"

He blinked hard, completely taken off guard. They hadn't ever talked about him not attending NYU. It was his dream school even if recently he had wondered about his choice.

"No, but there were great design schools in New York. It would have been easy, with your talent, to be accepted into any one of them."

She put down her knife and fork. "That is exactly my point. You never considered changing your plans. You always assumed I should change the direction of my life to suit you. I had an excellent opportunity with a full scholarship; why would I have turned that down just to be by your side?"

The challenge was in her voice and for the first time, he heard how arrogant he sounded, like she needed to follow him just so that they could continue their romance. He had been a class A jerk only seeing his side this entire time.

"I can't believe I expected you to change your dream. I'm so sorry." And he meant it from the bottom of his heart, but he couldn't change what he had done in his youth. All he could do was show her he was a better man today. A man who didn't have the expectation she'd pack up and follow him. Even the fleeting thought he'd had about her leaving the farm and moving to Dallas to work as a designer again was self-centered. He audibly groaned.

"Are you alright?" Genuine concern filled her soft-brown eyes. "Do you want to leave?" She held up her hand to get Maggie's attention.

He reached out and took it. "I'm fine other than I've just discovered I'm a stupid guy, so full of himself that I'm ashamed to even admit it out loud to you."

She laughed softly. "It's okay. I already knew you were a regular guy when it comes to some things—others, you're kinda special."

He perked up. She still thought he had some good qualities. Now he had to know what they might be so he could build on them. "Do tell?"

She shook her head from side to side with a huge grin. "Nope, you'll need to figure that out on your own."

And just like that they settled back into their comfortable banter but with a new awareness on his part that he needed to really think about what he wanted from Renee. Maybe not just her but other people in his life, like his parents, his brother, and co-workers. It was time to stop taking people for granted.

15

———

*H*ank enjoyed the remainder of dinner and conversation with Renee. It was easy and they talked about their favorite movies and books they'd read. Despite the almost twenty-year separation, he was happy to discover some of her favorite adventure movies were his too. He went to pay the check and she pulled it from his hand.

"After all the work you've put in on my farm the last two days, the least I can do is buy dinner." She nodded in the direction of two brown paper boxes on the table. "And dessert."

The spark in her eye told him she wasn't taking no for an answer so rather than debate it, he'd let it go. But the picnic was on him, and he planned on going all out with her favorite foods and beverages. One of the ways he could show her how much he cared was creating a very special memory.

He draped his arm around her shoulders, and she slipped hers around his waist as they strolled down Main Street. She tipped her head back. "Just look at those stars."

Their steps slowed and she pointed to the night sky. "Look, there's the Big Dipper."

She had always been good at finding the constellations. "Do you still have that telescope you got for Christmas one year?"

"I do, but it's kind of late to set that up."

He wondered if she was tired. It had been a very busy few days and besides the physical labor, there had been a bit of an emotional journey for them both. "How about we take it with us this Sunday and we can stargaze."

"I was thinking, how about we go on Saturday instead. On Sunday I wanted to sleep in. Not that I'm an old lady or anything, but six days a week I'm super busy and if we want to watch the stars, it'll be a late night, which will make for a long week ahead."

That made sense. Since coming home, he'd made it a point to have Sundays off. It helped him ease into the week, check work email, and basically used it as a low-key office day.

"Sounds like a great idea. Do you think we can head out by six? I'll be done with chores if you can wrap up your day too."

She held him a little closer and said, "Six it is. What should I pack?"

"Not a thing. I've got it covered."

"But...."

He dropped a kiss on her cheek. "The deal was you'd have to go on a picnic with me, not that you had to fill the basket too."

She smothered a yawn. "That's not how I understood it."

He turned them back toward his truck; tiredness was etched around her brown eyes. "My motivation for the deal was to spend time with you. I know you can cook, but you've got your hands full right now, so let me take care of it. You'll get it next time."

A jab to his heart made him wonder when the next time would be. Picnics weren't something that was a weekday kind of thing, unless they did it at the farm, and then he'd be shirking his responsibility at the ranch, despite what Dad said about firing him and getting back in the saddle.

He could see the smile quirk the corners of her mouth in the soft light of the streetlamp.

"If you insist, who am I to argue. But *can* you actually cook? In River Junction, you can't run down to a gourmet store and order a picnic basket to go; it's not like Dallas."

Hank chuckled. "Don't you worry. And FYI, I've actually learned how to cook quite well. I promise you won't go hungry and the flavors will dance across your taste buds."

"After a day in the field, I'll be starving and would eat just about anything in front of me."

He opened the passenger door and waited until she was sitting before leaning in. "Renee, the last three days have been the best I've had in a very long time. I'm going to have to give the cattle an extra ration of oats as thanks for helping us reconnect."

She tipped her head to the side and a slow smile slipped over her face. "When you put it that way, I guess it has been a pretty happy accident that the fence was down and they braved the river to find greener grass on the other side."

He cupped her cheek in his hand and lowered his lips to hers. "Sometimes old sayings are true." His lips lingered on hers; he was not ready for the evening to be over.

"What sayings aren't true?"

"That you can't go home again." He looked into her eyes. "Coming home, so many things are the same—and the best, unexpected surprise of all was you."

"I feel the same way. Spending time with you has been wonderful."

He could see the shutters roll down over her emotions as soon as the words left her mouth. He got it. She was scared. Unwilling to tear apart what they had begun to rediscover, he said, "Let's make our plans and stay in the moment. The future isn't important right now. I just want to spend time with you."

She brushed the hair from his forehead. "The future will come whether we obsess about it or not, but you're right—let's not think about it. I want to enjoy this time with you. I feel alive again. It's as if I've been living in some kind of gray haze and you've brought brilliant color back to me."

She said it perfectly.

His fog had lifted and he was seeing life more clearly. Not that he was ready to make a declaration.

"My life is better when you're in it, Renee." He kissed her one more time, slow and sweet, before it was time to drive her home.

The next morning, Hank strode into the kitchen and filled his mug with coffee, silently thanking his mom for setting the pot up last night.

"You're up early."

He spun around and his dad was sitting at the table. His cane leaned against the wall and a closed book was in front of him.

"Dad, I didn't think you or Mom would be up this early." He held up the coffee pot. "Care for a mug?"

"Please." Dad waited until Hank sat down. "What's eating you, son?"

"The dam is bugging me. I talked with Joe and he said it was carefully constructed of materials found from the land, almost as if it were beavers, but there was a complexity that shouts it was man-made. And I just don't get why."

"How far up was it located and who owns the land on the opposite side, us or the Mitchells?"

"We do and the funny thing is, the water that was diverted would mostly affect Renee's orchard if she needed to irrigate. The main offshoot still flows over the other pasturelands." He sipped his coffee. "I've got a bad feeling that someone is looking to harm the orchard, but for the life of me I couldn't say why. It's the third generation of Mitchells farming there and I've never heard of anyone saying a bad word about them."

Dad drummed his fingertips on the kitchen table. "There's one possibility that has to be talked about."

Hank lifted his head to study his father's face. "Which is?"

"Last fall, Dave mentioned Lucas Gasperini came around with an offer to buy the orchard. He has big plans to develop the area of River Junction and it was around the same time Renee decided to leave Chicago and buy the orchard from her parents. Gasperini was pretty offensive when talking about a woman living out there alone and attempting to run a farm. Almost as if he'd wait in the wings until she failed." He sat up straight in the chair and shook his head. "Son, you need to talk with Robert Adler. He handled the paperwork for the transfer of ownership to Renee."

"What could he tell me that wasn't confidential? With Renee being the owner and if things got rocky, she might be willing to sell out and maybe now the offer wouldn't be as generous. Drying up her orchard was a risk. If that was the plan, there would be no way he'd know if the weather would be hot and dry this year or if she'd need to irrigate."

His dad gave a chuckle. "You've been away from the ranch too long. With new trees, irrigation would be critical for success. Before it got cold, Dave noticed the change in the river and helped Renee set up an irrigation system as a backup. He understood not having a strong flowing river would have caused her a huge problem."

Hank ran his hand over the stubble on his chin and nodded thoughtfully. "Maybe I'll run into town today and see if Robert has a few minutes to chat. I'd like to know a little more about Lucas Gasperini and if Rob knows what the plans are for taking over the town. Also, it'd be helpful to know if anyone sold out yet."

The original Hank Shepard sipped his coffee. Over the rim, he gave Hank a serious look as his eyes narrowed. "I happen to know he approached John Grace from Grace Star Ranch and if you remember anything about John, he sent that man packing faster than a greased pig slides through hands at the county fair."

"I'd hazard a guess that Gasperini needs one of the larger ranches to become the cornerstone of this project and without us or Grace Star, he's lacking the leverage he really needs. So he set his sights on the orchard which borders our land." At least Hank hoped none of the other ranchers would sell out to this guy. "Have other businesses in town, like the Filler Up Diner or The Trading Post, been approached yet?" The more information he had, the better his questions would be when he spoke to Rob Adler.

"Not that I know of—and the orchard would be a good cornerstone. They have a lot of acreage and the location is excellent. Easy access to town, the river for fishing, some open land as well as the orchard. Setting up a luxury hotel there could be very enticing to guests, given the right amenities."

Hank pushed back from the table. "I'm going to eat breakfast and then head to town around seven thirty. On my way, I'll make a few stops, talk to folks, and see if anyone has anything to share about this guy and his plan."

"That's an excellent idea and while you're catching up

with Rob, maybe you can ask him what his plans are for retirement."

With a deep sign and a shake of his head, Hank said, "Dad, we're not going to cover that same ground, are we? I have a job in Dallas. That's where I live now; in fact, I have for years. I have a decent life there."

His dad's brow arched. "River Junction has a few things Dallas doesn't. Your family, horses, wide-open spaces, fresh air, a potential to be your own boss, and—"

Hank knew what was coming next. "I know what you're doing and it's not going to work."

"Do you think Renee would want to pack up and leave her business to be with you and as a not so gentle reminder, you did that once and lost her. I wouldn't suggest you try that again. This time she might not forgive you as easily."

With a snort, he said, "Do you think she's been that easy on me? I hurt that woman and after twenty years, she's finally decided we can spend time together. It wasn't like I didn't want to contact her before now. And I don't mean this in a bad way, but you breaking a hip was the best thing that could have happened. It brought me home and allowed me to rediscover my feelings for Renee."

It was his dad's turn to chuckle and he said, "Glad I could help you with your love life."

"Dad, you know what I meant." He said, "Just for that, you can help me convince Mom to whip me up a batch of those cowboy cookies Renee likes. On Saturday I'm taking her on a picnic."

With a wiggle of his bushy eyebrows, his dad wagged a finger in Hank's direction. "That's my son, trying to ply his girl with his momma's cooking. You did that same move when you were in high school."

With a laugh, he said, "Pop, if it ain't broke, why change it?"

16

*R*enee was up to her elbows in hot, soapy dishwater. Bubbles mounded on the windowsill and Ginny was withdrawing a cupcake tray from the oven. The kitchen had never smelled so scrumptiously good since her mom had lived there.

"Ginny, what's next after you're done with the apple butter cupcakes?" She liked that apple was the day's theme and glanced over her shoulder. "And before you answer that, I want to toss out an idea I had."

"What's on your mind?" She tapped on the top of the timer and closed the oven door, then gave her full attention to Renee.

"I know you have your current cookbook project to turn in, but what about, after you're done with that, maybe you could come up with some recipes that I could feature in my new store." She wiped her hands with the towel that rested on her shoulder. "Nothing major, just a few ideas to inspire more sales of the apple products I want to carry."

Ginny tapped the deep dimple in her cheek. "No. That's not a good idea."

Renee's stomach clenched and she dropped her gaze to

the floor. "Sorry. You're—" Before she could go any further in her comment, Ginny laughed.

"Silly, you need an entire apple-themed cookbook and I can self-publish it. Just think..." She gazed off as if looking into the future. "A Virginia Rhodes exclusive only available at River Bend Orchard. And if you want, maybe we could hold a cooking demonstration on a couple of weekends right after the bulk of the harvest has been picked."

Was Ginny saying she was interested or just tossing out a crazy idea so Renee would turn it down? "You want to dive in with me?"

Her brow went sky high. "Don't you remember back in college when we did that project about running a business together? Not that I want to become an apple grower, but if you're interested in collaborating, I could write a cookbook based on the products you plan on carrying and we can promote it like crazy. I'll bet that would bring folks in, the cooking demos. Heck, maybe we could be ready to do something really big during the height of tourist season."

Renee gulped back her surprise. "Like in three or four months? Do you have enough time to write an entire book with your current workload?"

"For this year, we could create just a couple of simple recipes, maybe some muffins and how to make an apple jam, and tease the cookbook for next season. This way we can try a few ideas out, maybe even test a couple of covers. You know, get shoppers to vote and if they do, we could have a contest and anyone who votes is entered to win a free autographed copy."

"Would something like that work?" A flicker of hope eased the knot in her gut. "The Virginia Rhodes cooking demos alone would certainly draw folks in, but would you really want to go all in and write an entire book on apples?"

"Absolutely. Not only will it justify me hanging around River Junction, but I could stretch my cooking chops thinking of all the ways to incorporate apples into meals three times a day plus sweets." With a tip of her head, Ginny smiled. "And the best part is we'd be working together on something that will generate income for both of us. Plus the added bonus, we'll be fulfilling that long-ago dream."

Taking a step toward Ginny, Renee extended her hand. "We'll shake on it for now, but I'll make an appointment with Robert Adler, the local attorney, and we'll make it official."

With a firm shake, the ladies grinned and in unison, they said, "Partners."

$\mathcal{L}$ater that afternoon, Renee and Ginny were in the living room, both reclining and watching an old Cary Grant movie when Ginny said, "I've been thinking. Do you really want to go to the expense of getting a formal contract for our JV?"

The question caught Renee off guard for half a second. "I would never want our joint venture of this new side hustle to cause friction between us. If we each know what is needed or expected, it gives us parameters to work between and hopefully this will grow into something larger. But will it be an issue, you releasing a cookbook as an independent author?"

"No. When you went out to inspect the field, I called my agent and told her what I was planning. A part of her was disappointed I wouldn't allow her to pitch it to the publishing house. But when I explained this project was very personal to me, all she asked was to be invited to the launch next year."

Renee wriggled up straighter on the chaise. "Really? Isn't that lost income to her if you go indie?"

With a grin, Ginny said, "I know how Marge's mind

works. Once word gets out next year and people start pouring into the orchard because of all the amazing products you have in the store, it will introduce people to my cookbook. Then once they fall in love with our concept, they'll want to buy more apple products and give them a reason to buy my other cookbooks. It's the trickle-down theory."

"That makes sense now." She chewed on her bottom lip. "You can change your mind if you spoke off the top of your head. I have no idea how sales will be and that's a lot of money out of your pocket to publish the new book."

With a small smirk, Ginny said, "And how would you know?"

She lifted her shoulder in a shrug. "You know I love to research so I went online and looked up what it takes to just get a book ready for publication—editors, proofreaders, photography, and then the printing cost. Just wow."

"That is all true but I've got connections within the industry and we'll have the best people on our team. Which is a good segue to my ideas about your website."

Renee felt her mouth dip into a frowny face. "What website?"

With a clap of her hands, Ginny said, "Exactly. When the photographer I want to hire comes out to take pictures of my recipes, I'm going to ask that he do a complete shoot of the orchard and the full operation. He'll need to come during picking season and when the cider press is in operation, but you need to create an online presence so people can order products from the website—my cookbook included."

"Aren't you gearing up to promote before the apples have even grown?"

Ginny tossed a throw pillow across the room. "Since when did you stop dreaming big?"

"Since I planted an entire field of trees only to have

them trampled and then had to replant, with more stock on the way to finish the project."

She wiggled her brow in Renee's direction. "Which brought a very handsome lawyer to your door along with what? Two dinner dates and soon-to-be a third, a riverside picnic."

Heat flushed her cheeks as Ginny ribbed her about Hank. She had been right; if it wasn't for the cattle getting into her field, she never would have spent any time with him and even though sadness hovered on the horizon, she was glad to have been able to let go of the past hurt.

Renee put her laptop aside and got up. "I'm going to fix dinner. Care to keep me company?"

Ginny did the same. "I'll help. That way we can start eating sooner, and I was thinking. Do you still have some apples in storage in the barn?"

They went into the kitchen and Renee took the chicken breast from the refrigerator. "I do. Are you thinking of trying a new idea?"

"How does savory apple stuffed chicken breasts sound?"

Renee grabbed her jacket and with her hand already on the doorknob, she grinned. "Like I'm headed to the barn. I'll be right back."

She closed the door and jogged across the gravel parking area, making a beeline to the barn. The sound of tires crunching the gravel caused her to stop and wait to see who would appear around the last bend of her driveway. Her heart rate quickened when she saw the sleek dark-gray Mercedes SUV ease to a stop close to where she stood. Her friends didn't drive that type of vehicle, at least not in this town. Back in Chicago had been a different story.

The man straightened his fedora and placed his sunglasses on the dashboard before the driver's door opened.

He was dressed in a dark-gray custom-cut suit with a pale-blue shirt and dark paisley tie, and black alligator boots. If the man was attempting to blend in and look like a local, he was off base. In that part of cowboy country, fedoras were for Indiana Jones, not John Wayne. She'd give him an A for trying too hard and a C for the overall look, minus the hat.

Planting both feet in a wide stance, as she finished grading his look, she asked, "Can I help you?"

"I'm looking for Renee Mitchell." He looked to her right and left. "Is she available to speak with me for a minute or two? We have an appointment."

With a suppressed smile and the upper hand, she asked, "Who's looking for her?"

With a slight nod to his head and a slick salesman smile she had seen a thousand and one times, he said, "Lucas Gasperini."

"You say you have an appointment with Ms. Mitchell?"

"Yes." The word stuttered as it came out. "Would you be able to call her for me? I'm running a little early."

Renee couldn't resist having a little more fun with this clown. "You don't say. About what exactly?"

"To discuss some mutual business." He took a step in the direction of the back door. "I'll just knock. If you'll excuse me."

"That won't be necessary."

As if on cue the back door opened and Ginny stepped out, looking first at Gasperini and then Renee. "What's going on out here?"

He stretched out his hand and hurried over the gravel to Ginny. "Ms. Mitchell, I'm Lucas Gasperini and I hoped you could spare a few minutes of your time for me. I'd like to discuss a business proposition with you."

She quirked a brow and looked at Renee as if asking should she play along with whatever was going on.

Renee held two fingers up and then down to the ground. It was an old signal they had used back in college when guys were hitting on them and the girls had zero interest in them. She was confident Ginny would have her back.

"I'm sorry but you're confusing me with the owner of this orchard. I'm an old family friend." She stepped to the top step, effectively blocking the entrance to the house.

"Mr. Gasperini."

He twirled on the heel of his boot and looked at Renee, his eyes narrowed. "You're Renee."

"Ms. Mitchell to you. Now you can state your business so I can decline your offer or you can just leave. My parents told me that you had offered to purchase the orchard before I returned to River Junction. It wasn't for sale then, and it's not for sale now."

He crossed the space between them and stopped directly in front of her. His face softened. He had moved on to his *I'm doing you a favor* look.

"An orchard is a lot for one person to handle and with planting all those new trees, it had to be expensive. What are you going to do if we don't get a decent amount of rain this year?"

"That isn't for you to worry about, Mr. Gasperini, but I happen to have an excellent irrigation system in place."

He handed her an envelope. "Just take a look at my offer and my phone number is in there. I can be reached day or night." He strode back to his SUV and paused before opening the door. "It would be a shame if Mother Nature didn't cooperate with you this season and I'm sure the neighboring ranch needs water for their cattle." He jerked open the door. "It's a fair offer. You'd be wise to consider it."

Renee wouldn't let him see that he had poked her one very tender nerve. "Please remove yourself from my property before I call the sheriff. Around here, we don't take kindly to trespassers, and next time you decide to drop in on someone, you might want to call first. This time of year, bears are waking up and landowners tend to be extra cautious about who or what roams their land."

The SUV roared to life and Gasperini gunned the engine and kicked up gravel as the tires spun when he backed around and raced down the driveway.

Renee looked at Ginny and exhaled. "I'll be right in. I still need to get the apples."

17

*H*ank took a stool at the counter. The Filler Up was jamming. All the booths and tables were full, and it was standing room only around the room. As he looked around, he recognized most of the faces of business owners and ranchers. Rocco Mills, owner of the local watering hole, The Lucky Bucket, set his coffee down on the counter and stood up.

"Thank you everyone for coming." With a nod, he acknowledged Hank. "For those of you who haven't been approached yet by a development company, we wanted you to be prepared. There has been a man nosing around town, making offers to buy ranches and other businesses. And don't misunderstand, we all need to do what is best for ourselves and our families, but a few of us thought we should talk about what is going on. I wanted to share my perspective."

Cora Davis, the branch manager of the bank, stood up. "Rocco, if I might jump in here."

He waved his hand in the direction of the people. "You have the floor."

She gave him a smile of thanks. "I would like to reassure

everyone that River Junction Bank will not share any of your personal information about loans or any financial information with anyone. I have had two phone calls from concerned customers asking why I gave out personal information to Mr. Gasperini. I can assure you, no one who works at the bank, myself included, would ever divulge one iota of information. If he insinuated otherwise, he's lying."

Becky Easton, whose family owned the bed and breakfast in town, leapt to her feet. She glared at Cora. "I was told you planned to sell our loan to one of his business associates."

"Untrue." Cora's gaze circled the room. "This is just the type of information that he seems to sprinkle around, getting you to believe him and then getting you to take an offer. If the deal he presents seems too good to be true, in my experience it probably is."

"Why would he tell me that?"

"It's a subtle pressure tactic, Becky," Hank interjected. "From a legal perspective, Cora's right. The bank can't give out your private information without your permission and if he is implying that happened, it's unethical. But there are times when developers create an illusion to get land and business owners to take whatever the offer might be. I would be wary of anything that he says."

Rocco said, "Thanks, Hank. For those of you who might think that guy looks familiar, he's Henry Shepard's son, the hotshot lawyer from Dallas."

He stood up. "I wouldn't say a hotshot, but yes, I'm an attorney and if you have questions, I'd encourage you to talk with Rob Adler."

Becky's eyes narrowed and she asked, "Has anyone approached your dad?"

"Yes, and he halted the conversation before Mr. Gasperini could even think to make an offer. Since I've been home, we've talked about what's been happening around town and Dad said he has no interest in selling the ranch. Period. And in full transparency, we just talked again about what is going on this morning and he reiterated that he has zero plans to sell."

A murmur of approval rippled through the group. A man Hank didn't know said, "Does anybody know if anyone has taken Gasperini up on his offer?"

No one spoke up, so either it hadn't happened or if it did, nobody wanted to spill the cider.

Another person asked, "Who else has something to say in regard to Gasperini or what could happen to the town if businesses start to sell out?"

Rocco's face morphed into a frown, and Hank felt the need to once again speak up.

"Just to be clear, everyone. If you are approached with what you think could be a favorable deal, make an appointment to discuss the terms with Robert Adler. He can make sure the contract doesn't have any surprises."

Jeremy Morgan jumped to his feet. "I won't be selling The Trading Post and if you're suggesting we should start talking to this guy, I want to know one thing. Has the heat in Dallas warped your brain?"

The conversation had taken an unexpected turn and Hank needed to nip it before it got out of hand. "I'm not suggesting that anyone or everyone sell their homes and businesses. But if a resident wants to, they certainly have that right. Just be proactive and protect yourself. There's no harm in me providing you with some prudent advice." He watched as the air of indignance seemed to deflate from Jeremy. "I might not live here but that doesn't mean I don't love this valley as much as you all do. This is where I grew up and someday, I hope to bring my kids here to learn to ride a horse and rope a cow. River Junction is special. I can understand why a developer would want to capitalize on our little slice of heaven."

Maggie shot him a grin from the other side of the diner and gave him a thumbs-up.

He was grateful that there was one person in the room who understood what he was trying to say. "I didn't mean to insert myself into your meeting and I apologize if you feel I overstepped."

Rocco grinned at his old friend. "You always did like to share your opinions, but in this case, Hank, I'm glad you were here. You gave excellent advice and it's good to know that we all should proceed with caution around this man. It seems he might have a bit of a problem with the full truth."

"Yeah, we don't have to like the man and he is just doing his job. I'm sure his high-pressure tactics have proven effective for him in the past."

Jeremy said, "Well, not this time and not in our town." He stood and looked at Maggie. "I'll buy Hank's breakfast today." He crossed the diner, winked, and shook Hank's hand. "Consider breakfast as payment for your hotshot legal advice."

"This is a first but glad I could help, Jeremy. And if you have any other questions and Rob is tied up, feel free to reach out. I'm always happy to help."

"You're a good guy. Thanks."

Patrons settled back in to order and enjoy breakfast and finally Maggie stood in front of Hank. "What'll it be today? I've got huckleberry pancakes and sausage."

Never one to turn down huckleberry anything, he grinned. "Just a short stack; this is my second breakfast."

Maggie ran her gaze down to his boots and with a laugh, she said, "You could use a third; you're too thin."

He dropped his voice and said, "If you repeat this, I'll deny it, but I forgot how hard it is to work on a ranch. I swear the weight has fallen off me since I got back."

She laughed even harder. "Now that makes sense." She tapped the counter in front of him. "Not to worry. I'll tell Mack to add some extra butter to your meal."

He shook his head. His weight might be down but his cholesterol was sure to skyrocket with all the hearty, rib-sticking food he'd been eating. There was nothing like eating his momma's home cooking or for that matter the meals in the hometown diner.

*H*ank strolled down Main Street, overfull from the pancakes—which was not a short stack—sausage patties, and two mugs of coffee he had savored at the diner. Other customers had stopped to chat or thank him for speaking up at their informal town meeting, and he was on his way to see Robert Adler, the town's only lawyer.

The law office was in an old farmhouse-style building with a wide wrap-around porch. The floor was painted a deep green with a sitting area with two sturdy mission-style rocking chairs and a matching side table. A spider plant cascaded to the floor and a few glossy magazines sat on the table as if just waiting for someone to kick back and relax. It was very inviting. Hank wondered if people waited out here in nice weather or if Robert came out during the day to take his coffee and recharge. If this was Hank's office he knew he'd want to take a break right here.

He stepped onto the wide wooden steps and turned to look over his shoulder. The town sprawled out in both directions, so this was a great location. The wood and beveled glass doors were a weathered aqua and looked original to the building. He clasped the black wrought iron lever doorknob and twisted it as it moved silently. Once inside, the wide pine floors were highly polished and a thick oriental rug in deep shades of red, gold, and black muffled his footsteps. The receptionist's chair was empty but a twirl of steam rose from the coffee mug on the desk. A murmur of voices drifted from down the hall and Hank took a seat in one of the cushioned leather chairs. He liked the vibe of the office—very classy while being comfortable and welcoming.

The sound of high heels clicking on the floorboards announced someone before he saw them. Getting to his feet, he smiled at the older woman. One of his mother's longtime best friends stood in front of him. "Mrs. McCarthy. It's good to see you."

"Hank Shepard." She gave him a warm hug. "Your mom said you were home but I'm surprised to see you here. I figured you had your hands full at the ranch, and please call me Corinne. Mrs. McCarthy makes me feel ancient."

"As of today, Dad took over at the ranch so I'll be heading back to Dallas next week. But I was hoping to talk with Attorney Adler if he has a few free minutes."

"Let me just tell him you're here." She gestured to the chair. "Make yourself comfortable and I'll be back shortly."

Instead of sitting, Hank made his way around the room. Paintings of the landscape around River Junction adorned the walls. He looked at the corner to see who the artist was and noted the initials RA. They were stunning and he even recognized the bend in the river near where the cattle had crossed to Renee's orchard.

"Admiring my little hobby, are you, Hank?" Robert Adler was dressed casually in a navy-blue sport coat, a yellow-and-blue-striped shirt, and dark jeans with black cowboy boots.

"You're very talented, Rob." He clasped the older man's hand and gave it a hearty shake. "Sorry to just show up without an appointment, but I was hoping to talk to you about a little situation and bring you up to speed on my morning since I encouraged a few people to reach out to you for advice."

Rob gestured in the direction of the hallway. "Let's go back to my office. Corinne, would you mind bringing in a carafe of coffee?"

She said, "Of course."

He placed a hand on Hank's shoulder. "I don't normally ask her to make it, but it sounds like we have a great deal to talk about."

18

$\mathcal{F}$riday morning, Renee lay snuggled under blankets, cozy in her bed. Propping herself up on a mound of pillows, she looked out the window. The early morning sky was a dusky gray and soon the sun would be inching upward. All she wanted to do was think of the other night and the way it felt to be in Hank's arms and taste his sweet kisses on her lips. Memories washed over her, back to a time when their love was fresh and heart pounding. Time spent with him was like nothing she had ever experienced since—and the other night what was left of the dam protecting her heart crumbled away, allowing the feelings she had worked so hard to suppress bubble to the surface. It had taken her a couple of decades, but she finally discovered love wasn't something to forget but to treasure. Even if nothing ever went any further between them, at least she remembered what it was like to love with her whole heart.

Her phone rang and she picked it up and checked caller ID. With a smile bursting across her face, she said, "How did you know I was thinking of you?"

Hank's low, smooth laugh caused a butterfly explosion in her stomach. How could that happen with just a laugh?

"I didn't wake you?"

"No, I was thinking about what a nice time I had the other night." No way was she going to confess she had been thinking about the past too. Living in the moment was all they really had.

"I was wondering if you had plans for today."

Her pulse quickened. Just the suggestion of plans had her sitting up straight. "I need to check on the new plantings and walk the fence line. Call it being overly cautious, but I want to make sure nothing toppled over."

"Are you questioning the skill of the cowboys who set the posts?"

She could hear the playful tease in his voice. "You know that I've always been the one to double- and triple-check everything. Why should the fence be any different?"

"True. Care for some company?"

He can't keep hanging out at the farm; doesn't he have things to do at Stone's Throw Ranch? She longed to say yes, but she didn't want to put him in a time crunch either. It was like that as teenagers. He'd get up early and rush through his chores just to spend the day with her.

"I'd like that, but I've taken up a lot of your time with my problems, of which you've solved most of them. Thank you again. Besides, I need to run into town and talk with Robert Adler." She took a moment to slow her breathing. "But maybe we could meet when I get back,—have a late lunch?"

"What do you need to see Rob for, if I'm not overstepping. Is everything alright?"

With a laugh, she said, "I see your overprotectiveness sneaking out. Ginny and I are putting together some ideas for my country store and I want to have a partnership agreement in place to protect us both."

"I'd love to hear more about the plans and checking with Rob is an excellent idea. If you have any questions, let me know. I happen to be tight with a pretty good attorney."

"I'll keep that in mind. Now, are you up for lunch or do you have too much going on at the ranch?"

"You think I have stuff to get done here but"—he paused—"Dad fired me. Told me I was done filling in for him so I'm at loose ends for the next couple of days. If you need some help over there, I've got two idle hands."

Her heart soared and it didn't matter that he implied he had time before heading back to Dallas. They'd be able to spend time together. "Sounds good."

For a brief moment she wondered if maybe they could try something long distance. It wasn't like she had met anyone else she wanted to date, and some time with Hank was better than being without him. "In that case, do you want to head over in about an hour? We'll check out the new fields and you can ride with me into town. After that, I'll play hooky for the rest of the day."

"Now you're talking." His voice got a little amped. "And we can do anything you want today. So give it some thought."

"I will." She laughed softly. "See you soon."

She flung back the blankets and her feet hit the cool pine floor. The reflection in the mirror was the girl she remembered; deep-red hair framed her face which now had a few fine lines around her eyes—smile lines was what Mom called them—and a smattering of light freckles sure to deepen in the coming summer months. She was a few pounds heavier than in college, but she'd worked hard to not get too curvy. It wasn't a vanity thing but for good health, and now that she was actually working outside all day, she was seeing muscle definition that hadn't been there in years. Even if she'd been around the sun more times than she wanted to admit, it was pretty obvious Hank still found her attractive.

Time hadn't hurt him one bit. He was lean and muscular, but it was the kindness in his caramel-brown eyes that she always thought of first.

She padded into the empty kitchen and brewed a large pot of coffee. There were a few last-minute details she wanted to jot down about her agreement with Ginny before checking the forecast and email. The delivery of the cider press parts were due tomorrow which was a good thing since they needed to finish that before moving on to the next project on the list. And now with planning for cooking demonstrations, she and Ginny needed to design an area to accommodate tables and chairs. The list was never ending, but she had taken on the farm with enthusiasm despite the challenges she might face. Her plan had taken a few years longer than she thought, to build up her savings to make the leap. But the timing worked out perfectly with her parents' plans to retire.

Ginny came into the kitchen, her hair sticking up around her sleepy face. She yawned and headed straight for the coffee pot and grabbed one of the mugs sitting next to it. Mornings were not her best time and Renee knew it wasn't until her first mug was half-gone that actual words would come from her lips.

Ginny eased into a chair at the kitchen table, and holding the mug with both hands, she brought it to her lips and sipped. "Did you know I have a severe allergy?"

Renee paused in what she was writing and looked up. "No. Whatever it is, I'll make sure it stays out of the house."

With another long sip, Ginny's eyes focused on her. "If only you could fix this but sadly, it's an impossible feat."

Renee placed a hand on her arm. "What is it?"

"I'm allergic to the hours between midnight and eight in

the morning. And you have this strange habit of getting up with the sun."

She shuddered and Renee laughed. "I'm sorry that I woke you. I'll be quieter in the morning."

Lowering the mug to the table, Ginny shrugged. "It's okay, my dad used to say that I wasted the best part of the day by sleeping in. Who knows? Maybe the old sweetheart was right." She held up her hand. "But if you ever tell him I said that, I'll deny it."

"If it makes a difference, from November through February, I got up around eight. There's nothing that can be done outside so I take advantage and sleep in."

"Apparently my timing is awful. I should have made the move west sooner." She glanced at the pad in front of Renee. "What are you working on?"

"I'm writing down our plans for the country store. I'm going to talk with Robert Adler this morning and ask him to draw up some ideas for a contract that we can review next week—and of course you can send it off to your lawyer to check it too." She slid the pad across the table. "Take a look while I run through the shower. Hank's coming over and he's going to ride into town with me before I check the fence lines, and then we're going to have lunch."

Ginny wiggled her eyebrows. "Then I'll make myself scarce which works out great. I was going to get more supplies from the market today and spend the rest of the afternoon developing recipes for the cookbook. I only need a couple more, then I can send it in. There will be plenty if you want to have Hank come for dinner. I can hide out upstairs."

"No need to hide. I'll ask him and if he says yes, we'll all have dinner together. Maybe we can pitch our idea to him and see if he has any suggestions." Renee got up from the table. "I'll be down in fifteen minutes or less."

"Okay, if I think of something, I'll add it in the margins and take off before Hank gets here. Now that we're having dinner, I need to get a jump on the day so the kitchen doesn't look like a bomb went off when you two get back."

Before Renee got to the hall, she said, "You're pretty confident Hank is going to want to have dinner with us."

"It's not the *us* part; you're the only attraction." She pointed to the stairs. "Put on an extra swish of mascara too and make those eyes pop."

"It's not a date, Ginny, just two old friends hanging out."

"Keep telling yourself that, Ree."

Ginny's laughter followed her up the stairs.

*W*hen Renee came back down, Ginny was still at the table in her pj's with the notepad in front of her. Without looking up, she said, "Can we go over this before you head into town?"

"Sure." Renee pulled out a chair. She noticed the writing down both margins of the pad. Ginny had been busy.

"I've thought about this in a couple of phases spaced out over the next three years, and if you agree, we can set things in motion as soon as our agreement is signed."

Renee leaned back in her chair. Elated didn't begin to describe how she felt. Ginny was totally on board with the new venture. "I just want to say I'm thrilled that you're thinking long term and that you weren't offended I wanted a formal agreement. Too many times people have gone into business together without a plan and their friendship was crushed. I don't want that to happen to us."

Ginny nodded. "I agree and now for the fun part—and of course we can change any of this that you think is too much, too fast, or whatever."

She stood up and paced the length of the kitchen and

then back again. "Year one, also known as this fall,"—she grinned—"we host four cooking classes the last two weeks of September and first two weeks of October, one class per week. This will capture the mid and early part of the late-season varieties' harvest when the orchard should be at its busiest. I'd like to have the classes easy enough for kids, say ten and up, to enjoy and we'll make one recipe a week featuring whatever is the best apple at that current time, so of course that will be defined at a later date. In addition, I know you have apple cider donuts made here during the season, but I would like to introduce a baked donut as well. Some folks might not be able to eat a fried treat but baked could be an option."

Renee had flipped the pad open to a fresh page and was jotting notes as fast as Ginny spoke. "That's a great idea. I never had the bandwidth to do that. But that will take ovens. I'll need you to take a look at the space I've designated as the kitchen and see if it is adequate."

"That's easy enough." She snapped her fingers. "Do you have sales figures from the last couple of seasons? We're going to need to hire staff to keep the donuts coming fresh and warm during the day while you're open."

"I do." Renee flipped the page back. "It says here apple jam and butter."

"Right. I'm going to develop a unique spice blend for the apple butter, and I have some ideas about an apple caramel jam. For this year, we'll stick with the apple theme but down the road, I was hoping we could talk about planting huckleberry bushes. To keep folks spending money, you'll need a larger inventory of jams and other sweets. But again, that's year two and when the cookbook will be released—we'll again have four cooking classes, but they will be different from this season."

"And the third year?" Renee asked as the air of excitement wrapped around her like a comforting bear hug.

Ginny held up her arms in triumph. "The First Annual River Bend Orchard Apple Festival Dinner hosted by Renee Mitchell. Menu TBD."

With a clap of her hands, Renee jumped up and flung her arms around Ginny who hugged her tight. "When you dream, you go all in. But I like it. We can get started as soon as I'm back from town."

"After you stroll around the orchard and we have dinner with your handsome cowboy." With a saucy wink, Ginny sauntered from the room.

If Renee had any doubts about the long-term success of the orchard, Ginny had zapped them with her vision of what the future could look like. With a quick twirl around the kitchen table, she slipped the notepad into her bag. She wanted to make sure she gave Mr. Adler all the details so the partnership agreement would put her and Ginny on a level playing field.

19

*A*n hour later, Renee was locking the kitchen door when the crunch of tires on stone caught her attention. She smiled. Hank was five minutes early. She walked to the edge of the porch, surprised to discover it wasn't a truck but a dark SUV, its windows darkened with that special film that gave people inside privacy and protected them from the hot sun. Gasperini. Her stomach clenched and she wished Ginny was still home. But she could handle Gasperini by herself.

This time a driver got out from behind the wheel and opened the back passenger door. The older man got out and looked around. She knew he was taking in everything—the faded paint on the barn, the ancient tractor parked under the lean-to roof, and the house which also needed a fresh coat of paint. Her back stiffened and she thrust her chin up slightly. The new tree stock came before cosmetic touches.

Finally, he turned and acknowledged her with an arrogant nod.

She strode down the steps to where the man stood. "Mr. Gasperini, how may I help you today?"

"Ms. Mitchell, it's a pleasure to see you again." Lucas

Gasperini extended his hand and gave hers a limp shake. "I'm pleased to discover you're home today. I wanted to apologize for our last meeting. I know I upset you."

She ignored the urge to wipe her hand on her jeans and instead stuck it in her pocket, keeping her face neutral. "Don't give it another thought, I haven't. How can I help you?"

"I'd like to buy your farm and it's my understanding you're the sole owner since your parents retired."

She was trying desperately to remember what her parents said when they mentioned his name, but she was coming up blank. "You want to buy my farm, but it's not for sale."

"A minor detail." He unfolded a piece of paper and handed it to her. "As you can see, my offer is quite generous and it would give you an opportunity to purchase a lovely home and live very comfortably for the rest of your life."

She glanced at the number and then did a double take. There were digits that she hadn't ever seen coupled together on a farm offer. Not that she wanted to sell her family's living legacy, but she had a moment of pause. "This is an amazing offer but why do you want to purchase my orchard so badly?"

"You misunderstand. It's not the orchard I'm interested in acquiring. I'll have the orchards removed. The land is more valuable to me without it."

He stated it so matter-of-factly it was almost underwhelming.

"There is significant potential to develop an entire town devoted to a resort. Shops, restaurants, hotels, even to experience ranch life firsthand. I want to buy your property as a cornerstone for it all and before anyone else has the chance to stake a claim."

"Mr. Gasperini, thank you for your interest, but River

Bend isn't for sale. I'm surprised you were so forthcoming with why you want the land. I'm sure you understand. As far as constructing a resort town from a working ranch community, that's crazy. You really can't expect to swoop in here and buy up huge tracts of land and build. It will change the entire rhythm of the town and the reason why you think people would want to come here on vacation."

"In my line of work, I've discovered brutal honesty is the only way to conduct business. If I convince you to sell your farm and you found out after the fact I removed the orchard, well, that would sully my reputation and that would be intolerable to me. You might not appreciate my tactics, but I have ethics."

Renee looked away from Gasperini and exhaled. She was relieved to see Hank's truck come around the last bend in the drive. After all, he was a lawyer and maybe Gasperini would realize she meant what she said—there would be no sale of River Bend Orchard.

She held up her hand with a wave as he got out of the truck. "Hank."

Mr. Gasperini looked him up and down. He seemed to take note of his dusty boots, faded jeans, red plaid shirt, and tan cowboy hat.

Hank closed the distance between them and reached her side, touching the back of her arm with a light squeeze of support. "Renee, I didn't realize you were expecting anyone this morning."

His words were carefully measured, and she guessed this was how the lawyer in him sounded.

"I wasn't. Mr. Gasperini has made another offer to purchase the orchard from me." She handed him the slip of paper with the amount.

His expression never changed. "Mr. Gasperini, I'm sure Ms. Mitchell has told you her orchard isn't for sale and there are other larger orchards which might be a better investment."

With a dismissive wave of his hand, he said, "I don't give a fig about the orchard; in fact, I detest anything apple. My interest is the land." He waved his hand around. "All of this would be bulldozed."

Renee suppressed a gasp. The callous way he said he was going to destroy her orchard made her stomach turn. She clasped her trembling hands in front of her. "Hank, he's interested in developing the entire town into a resort area."

He gave her a side-look. "And what was your response? Is this something we should discuss?" He stuck out his hand to Mr. Gasperini. "Hank Shepard, I'm Ms. Mitchell's attorney."

His eyes widened for a fraction of a second, and if Renee hadn't been watching, she would have missed it.

"I was about to tell Mr. Gasperini my home is not for sale, at any price."

He gave a brisk nod. "You could check around with other family-owned businesses, but I think you'll find most people around here aren't quick to part with a living legacy."

"You would pass up on a very comfortable and early retirement?" Mr. Gasperini's gaze never left her.

"I'm not ready to give up on my dream and challenges. I'm proud to be a small woman-owned business." She gave his hand a firm shake. "Thank you for your interest, but no thanks."

If anyone thought she was a pushover, they'd better think again. If there was one thing she knew from growing up here, it was that Montana could chew you up and spit you out. Heck, that had been the same when she was in Chicago, but this was different. River Junction was her home and she wasn't going to sell—no matter how much money someone offered her.

Mr. Gasperini took a few steps toward the SUV door and paused. Looking at her with a steady glare, he said, "You could name your price, you know."

She lifted her chin and never blinked. "My home is priceless."

He tipped his head to one side before getting in the vehicle. As fast as he came, he left.

She exhaled the breath she didn't know she had been holding. "Can you believe that guy?"

Hank slipped an arm around her waist and held her close to his side. If he could feel her shaking, he didn't mention it. "You were amazing. Other people would have given that amount of money a second and third thought before turning him down flat."

"Would you sell off Stone's Throw Ranch for a big payday?"

Without a moment's hesitation, he said, "Absolutely not. Three generations of Shepards have worked hard to make the ranch what it is today. Selling out would mean their work was for nothing."

They stood watching the taillights as the SUV rounded the corner.

"Renee, don't be alarmed but I'm pretty sure he'll be back. I found out yesterday from Rob Adler there is good reason to think Gasperini is responsible for damming up the river. He was taking a risk. If the summer turns hot and dry and you don't have access to enough water to irrigate the trees, you'll get desperate and sell. From what Rob said, he thinks if you sell your property, it would cause a cascade effect with other tracts of land."

"Then Lucas Gasperini isn't an astute businessman after all. He's setting himself up to fail. Even if I had to truck in water, there is no way I'd let the trees die. I intend to make this orchard into a must-see destination for several reasons.

And with Ginny and me working together, we'll be unstoppable."

He nodded and said, "I have no doubt that you will accomplish all your goals."

She appreciated his support. "Now that we've had our excitement for the day, are you ready for boring errands and wandering in the fields?"

He dropped his lips to hers. "I can't wait. Time with you is never boring."

*H*ank was behind the wheel since he volunteered to drive into town and it gave Renee time to go over her notes. She looked his way; his profile was a sight she never tired of—his strong jawline and full lips always ready with a quick smile or hearty laugh.

He glanced at her. "Your smile is so wide it's like you have the best secret in the world."

"Not really, I was looking at you—remembering how many times we rode around in your truck, just like this."

"Good times." His voice held a touch of nostalgia. "There are things from our past I wish I could change."

She folded her hands in her lap. "Wishing won't change what happened. All we have is what we do from this moment forward. Can we live in the present and not worry about the future either?" If she was honest, she wasn't looking forward to when he got on that plane. This time would be harder, there was no anger involved. They had gone into seeing each other, knowing there was a ticking clock on their reunion.

Briefly, he touched her clasped hands. "You're right. We've dealt with our past and our roles in it and living in the present is much more enjoyable." They drove for a couple of minutes in silence until he said, "Will you continue to have Sunday dinner at my parents' once a month? I know they really like it when you do."

"Of course I will. It helps me miss my parents a little less and other than Ginny's cooking, it's the best food I get. Which reminds me, Ginny is cooking dinner tonight and asked if you'd join us. If you don't have other plans, that is."

He grinned. "I was hoping to just keep the day rolling right into the night. Do we need to stop off and get a bottle of wine, hard cider, or some other beverage?"

She shot him a grin. "I've got tonight covered since you have our picnic tomorrow."

He pulled up and parked in front of the sign that said Robert Adler, Attorney at Law. "Then it's another date."

Renee's tummy flipped over. It would be another night to remember, of that she was sure.

20

*L*ater that afternoon, Hank walked alongside Renee, holding her hand as they inspected the fence line. He didn't doubt everything would be exactly as they had left it, but he was with the woman he loved and it didn't matter what she wanted to do. By her side was the only place he wanted to be. Now that his dad was back in the saddle at the ranch, Hank had nothing to do but think about his future. Maybe that was all part of his dad's plan.

He was a lawyer and he passed the bar in Montana, but would practicing law in his hometown be fulfilling? After talking with Rob Adler, he learned there was more to legal affairs in River Junction than writing wills or reviewing basic real estate transactions. It was a slower pace than his practice in Dallas. There was something to having balance with work and a personal life. As they walked, he had to admit his life in Texas was empty and it didn't matter if he tried to convince himself a long-distance relationship would work. Talking on the phone, texting, or video calls would never fill the void he'd feel with Renee here and him there.

The warmth from their intertwined fingers filled his

heart. *This is what life should be about, walking hand in hand, doing mundane tasks that seem like perfection.*

She gave him a sidelong look. "What are you thinking about? You have a silly smile on your face, kind of like you got the last piece of huckleberry pie at Maggie's diner."

He lifted her hand and kissed the back of it. "I was thinking how it doesn't matter what we do. As long as we're together, I'm happy."

Her face softened and her eyes misted over. She had always been tenderhearted and that was just one of the many qualities he loved about her.

Her face screwed up in a quizzical look. "I'll have to admit I'm curious." They continued to walk at a leisurely pace, but she wasn't looking at the fence or him. "What are we doing? I mean, don't get me wrong. I love being with you, and it's stirred up strong feelings I thought were long gone, but what happens when you leave? I'm not looking for fluffy romantic promises, but do we agree to enjoy what we have now and stay friends, keep in touch with the occasional phone call or email, and exchange cards for birthdays and holidays? Is that how you want this to end?"

The air was sucked from his lungs. How could she think this was just some kind of an interlude and not the real deal between them? "That was a lot of questions, but would you prefer that we just keep our relationship as friendly and not explore what the possibilities might be?"

"Hank, that's completely illogical. We live fifteen hundred miles apart; it's not like we'll be getting together on weekends after a couple hours of windshield time."

He stopped walking and stepped in front of her to take both her hands in his. "These last weeks with you have shown me one thing: I have never stopped loving you or wanting you in my life. You're the beat of my heart and without you I'm like the Tin Man. You brought the sunlight and stars back into an overcast existence. It took coming home and having some cows lead me back to you to realize the truth."

He could see confusion cloud her eyes and he under-stood how she felt. He'd been wrestling with this for the last twenty-four-plus hours. "I thought we could hang out and be friends, just like when we were kids. Have some fun and enjoy spending time together, but I have to be honest and ask if you feel the same."

"Are you asking me if I still have strong enough feelings for you to have a long-distance relationship?" She pulled her hands away and walked a few paces down the path, her gaze seeming to focus on the freshly planted trees, but he knew better. She was putting distance between them to think.

He knew in that instant what he wanted. "Yes, I am. I don't want us to lose contact again—at least until we figure out a longer-term solution. I want us to talk often and see each other when we can. I'll talk to the partners and see if it's feasible to work remotely. If I'm not due to appear in court, maybe I can steal away for some long weekends over the next few months. It's not ideal but at the very least it's a start." His heart hammered in his chest; he longed for her to say it's what she wanted too.

With a heavy sigh, she said, "A long-distance relation-ship won't be easy. I've had friends who tried and it didn't work out. Instead of putting a label on whatever we might have now or in the future, we should agree to maintain our very strong friendship and see how it grows."

It wasn't exactly what he had in mind, especially since kissing her and holding her in his arms was not a friend kind of a thing. But if that was as far as she was willing to go right now, then he'd accept her terms. In a few long strides he was next to her. He wanted to take her hand but didn't want to come off as pressuring her to see their rela-tionship the way he did. "Renee, if that's what you want, then that's what we'll do. We'll take it slow but please know I'm committed to making this work."

She threw her arms around his neck and hugged him tight. With a catch in her voice, she said, "Don't misunderstand. I have very deep feelings for you but I'm scared to death we'll hurt each other again and I couldn't bear it. Losing us once was painful; losing us twice would be excruciating."

He inhaled the sweetness of her vanilla shampoo and sun-dried clothes. This was his very special Montana memory and one he'd carry with him on the plane. A lump lodged in his throat. *How am I going to get through every day without seeing her smile or holding her?* It hadn't taken long for him to wake each morning looking forward to seeing her beautiful face.

He held her a little tighter until she said, "Are you trying to commit this moment to memory or can we get back to our walk?"

The lightness in her tone didn't hide the deep emotion in her words.

He relaxed his arms and placed a kiss on her temple. She felt so right in his arms he wasn't ready to let her go.

"Let's finish checking the new trees so we can spend the rest of the day having fun. I was thinking we could go for a trail ride later and then have dinner with Ginny."

"That sounds nice." She cupped his cheek in her hand and looked deep into his eyes. His heart did a somersault in his chest. "You are a very special man, Hank Shepard, and I'm glad we've had this time together."

Throwing a saddle blanket over the back of a mare, Renee called out, "What's her name again?"

With a chuckle, he said, "Dolly and she's partial to apples—carrots not as much."

He came out of the tack room with a saddle for Ranger and set it on the stand before going back into the tack room to get Renee's.

When he returned, she blinked hard and stared at the saddle Hank held in his hands. Her mouth gaped open, then with a stammer, she said, "You... You still have my saddle?"

He was glad he had chosen this as a surprise. It was the saddle he had bought for her sixteenth birthday.

She ran her fingertips over the hand-tooled leather embellished with flowers and an intricate basket weave pattern, then over the suede padded seat. "I adore the silver conchos and plates. It's still a work of art."

"Of course I kept it. I would never get rid of it." He placed it on Dolly's back and tightened the girth strap.

"I figured it was long gone." She traced the tooled roses as if seeing them for the first time. "I always wondered...."

Her words trailed off and she didn't finish the sentence, but he knew. He had often thought he should have dropped it by her parents' place. They had horses too, but this had been their special outing they did at his parents' ranch—saddle up and ride. The only downside were the mounts they used to ride had long since gone over the rainbow bridge, but he would never have gotten rid of her tack. In his heart he dreamed he'd ride with Renee again and now it was his reality.

They finished getting the horses ready when he heard his mom calling to them.

"In the barn," he yelled over his shoulder.

She entered carrying a wicker basket. "Hello, you two. I thought you'd like to take a light lunch with you."

Renee stepped around Dolly. "Hi, Maeve. I don't think we'll be gone long so a picnic wasn't necessary."

Hank said, "Hold on. I'll get a saddle bag to carry everything." He stepped into the tack room, leaving the two women. He could hear Renee thank his mom for everything. When their voices dropped too low for him to hear, he paused, giving them another moment. Curious, he went back in.

"Are you two sharing secrets about this handsome rancher?" He gave Renee an exaggerated wink.

"Someone thinks very highly of himself." His mom gave Renee a one-armed hug. "Good luck, Renee; his head might not fit through the barn door."

"Mom." He held his hand up and pointed to his chest. "Family loyalty."

"Son, sometimes the truth is too important to hide." She fluttered her fingers as she walked out the door, laughing as she slid it closed.

Once the saddle bags were filled and secured in place on Ranger's backside, they walked the horses into the paddock. The sun was reaching its peak. It was going to be a spectacular trail ride. The sky was clear, and the air was cool. Originally, Hank thought it was the perfect afternoon for lazing in the sunshine and fresh air, a few sweet kisses, and stolen glances but given their conversation earlier, he'd have to play it cool and do his best to turn up the romance.

Holding Dolly's reins, Renee swung a leg up and leaned over the mare's neck to whisper in her ear. She grinned at him. "We're just getting acquainted before we spend time together."

He mounted Ranger and settled in with a light tap of his heels. The quarter horse moved to the gate where Hank leaned over and unlatched it. Dolly kept pace with Ranger and by the smile on Renee's face, she was already relaxed and having a good time. Once the gate was secured, the horses eased into a trot and it was easy to see that Renee hadn't lost her grace in the saddle.

She flashed him a grin, adjusted her cowboy hat, and tapped her heels to the mare's sides; the horse broke into a light lope. Renee's deep-red hair flowed in the breeze, her musical laughter reaching his ears. Today was just what they needed.

After about thirty minutes they reached a stand of pines, pulled the horses up, and dismounted, looping the reins around a low branch.

She patted Dolly's neck. "This is a great spot. We can watch the fish leap in the river. Too bad we didn't bring poles."

He gave her a gentle shoulder bump. "I'm holding out for some R & R time."

Color flushed high in her cheeks. She pulled a blanket roll from the back of her saddle and flicked it out to cover the scrubby grass. "Are you building a fire?"

"Of course. Help me gather some wood?" He held out his hand to her and he was pleased she took it without hesitation.

After they had gathered enough wood for a decent fire, he lit the dry sticks and within minutes it glowed with red and orange flames. The air was cool, but near the fire they'd be warm.

With the flames crackling and casting a warm circle and the remnants of lunch spread out around them, they reclined on the blanket. The sun was already beginning its journey to the west. It seemed like they had already run out of things to say, but he had much to talk about.

"Do you remember when we were teenagers and the first time our dads let us go on an evening trail ride?" He covered her hand and gave it a squeeze.

She laughed. "Dad was at the ranch when we got back with the flimsy excuse that he needed to talk about a load of manure for our garden. Like we needed an entire honey wagon for a ten-by-twenty-foot area."

"I remember that and when I said I was driving you home, the look on their faces was priceless, as if you were going to end our date being driven home by your dad."

"After that I guess they figured we knew what we were doing, riding after dark, but wow, they were so transparent. Yet we all knew it was much more than a ride." She leaned in and kissed his cheek. "Today when we get back, our fathers won't be waiting for us."

She was breathtaking. "Oh good, then taking you home won't be a problem." He lowered his lips to hers.

21

*R*enee looked at the clock, wishing that time would slow to a crawl, at least for today. It was Hank's final morning, and they were going to spend it together with a leisurely picnic and some quiet time before he headed to Bozeman to catch his late-night flight.

Last night had been wonderful. In looking back over the last several weeks, every minute with him had been special and she wished they had gotten together when he first came to town instead of her doing her best to be invisible to him. However, the circumstances of them reconnecting couldn't have been forced; it needed to be organic after all this time—and totally unexpected was the best way possible. Thank goodness for cattle wanting to munch on greener grass.

Midmorning, she looked out the kitchen window and saw Hank's truck parked in her driveway. He sat staring straight ahead. His face was drawn and pinched and looked as if he'd lost his best friend.

Her gut tightened as she watched him, obscured by the kitchen window. She knew how he felt since the sadness and emptiness had engulfed her several times this morning.

She plastered a smile on her face, determined to not let tomorrow's heartache infringe on today's happiness. Life was better when you had someone special in your life, especially a man like Hank Shepard—no matter how temporary.

She opened the kitchen door when he got out of the truck.

His eyes lit up when they met hers and his steps quickened, reaching her in a few long strides. He pulled her into his arms and crushed her to his chest.

She felt him take several slow, deep breaths, then he ran his fingertips over the curve of her cheeks and traced her lips before his touched hers again.

She savored the feel of his kiss, missing it and him already. Easing back, she said, "Are you all packed?"

Clouds seeped into his eyes. "Yes."

Her breath caught. They hadn't talked about when he was coming back to Montana, and she wanted to ask but didn't want to appear clingy and needy.

Slinging an arm around her shoulders, he steered her to the porch swing. "We have a couple of hours. What do you want to do? Walk, horseback ride, ATVs? Just name it."

"Let's walk down to the river and make sure the cows are staying on their side, and then I thought we could have our picnic in the hayloft."

He gave her a wide-eyed stare. "We fixed the fence." And then he grinned. "I see what you're doing, just poking at me." He pulled her close and kissed her forehead. "I'm going to miss this."

Softly, she said, "Me too." She took his hand and they strolled in the direction of the field before she changed direction and headed to the barn. "I want to show you something." It was an idea she'd had buzzing around her head, and she decided to bounce it off him.

They entered the dimly lit barn with the sun at their

backs. Leaving the doors wide open, she crossed to an interior room. She flicked the light on. It illuminated shelves where rows of jars with bright-red labels sat. The writing couldn't be seen from the doorway. She gave him a small smile. He was the first person she'd shared it with other than Ginny.

"I wanted you to see the genesis of the expansion. Besides the pick-your-own apples and cider for the fall season. I found my grandmother's apple butter and caramel apple jam recipes so last year I made some. With Ginny's expertise, we can expand into more jams and jellies and the cooking classes." She gestured to the shelves. "This has been my testing lab to see how they hold up to storage."

"Where is Ginny? I didn't see her SUV when I pulled in."

"She had a meeting." Renee didn't like that she fibbed to Hank, but Ginny had decided since today was their last day together, she'd make herself scarce and go house hunting. "With a real estate agent." Now there wasn't a lie hanging between them.

"Good for her." He crossed the room and picked up a jar. He turned. "Have you been holding out on me? I knew you were looking to grow your business, but I had no idea you made this kind of stuff. I thought this was going to be Ginny's department."

"It will be. This is last year's attempt." She chuckled. "Don't get too excited; you haven't tried it yet."

"Do you have crackers, biscuits? Heck, just a spoon will work." He picked up a jar and waved it toward the door. "Lead the way to the kitchen." He grabbed another jar so now he had one of each.

She wanted to skip her way across the driveway, thrilled he hadn't said the idea was a bad one and that he wanted to sample them. She'd been eating the delicious spreads all winter and they were holding up perfectly. Even Ginny thought they were a great beginning and Renee had agreed she could tweak the recipe to make it truly unique to the store.

The old-fashioned kitchen suddenly felt cozy with Hank in it. She gestured to the table. "Make yourself comfortable."

He pulled out two chairs and took one. "I've always liked this house; it welcomed me like it was my second home."

She glanced over her shoulder as she withdrew a box of crackers from the cupboard. "You spent enough time here growing up."

"That's what happens when your childhood friend morphs into the girl next door."

He winked and her pulse quickened.

She crossed the room and plunked the box of crackers in the middle of the table. Once the jars were opened, she placed several crackers on each paper napkin.

She put a hand on his. "Now, you have to promise to be honest. If you don't like one or both, you have to tell me. I want to expand what I can sell and longer term even have a mail order business if this takes off."

"I'm impressed how you're planning for the future." He scooped up the apple butter first and slathered the cracker so Renee could only see the apple mixture and popped it in his mouth. He closed his eyes and chewed very slowly.

She jabbed him in the side. "It's not like you have to chew your food for a minute before swallowing."

Without commenting, he repeated the process with another cracker.

Only this time she saw the twinkle in his eyes. "Hank, come on, tell me what you really think."

He wiped the crumbs from the corner of his mouth. "It's very good."

She waited for him to elaborate and when he didn't, she jabbed his ribs again.

He clutched his side as if she had caused him a severe injury. "What was that for?"

"It's just good, is that it?" She had played with a combination of cinnamon and nutmeg to try and mimic the flavors of apple pie and in each batch, she had used a different variety of apples. This particular one was a blend to achieve a sweetness without adding sugar. After all that tinkering, she thought it was perfect.

"You're impatient today. Chill and I'll tell you what I think after I try the jam for a second time."

After about five minutes of Hank tasting and re-tasting each jar multiple times, he grinned.

"I can't tell you which one is my favorite; I love the complexity of the apple butter with the spices and richness of the apple texture, but then the jam has the flavor of a great caramel apple without the stickiness that comes with it. Did you create these recipes yourself or use ones your mom had?"

"No, remember I mentioned these were my grandmother's. I started with her basic idea and then after making multiple batches of each, these were my favorites. I sent a couple of jars of each batch to my parents, just to see what they thought, and these were their favorites too."

"Where do you go from here? Have you written a formal business plan for the expansion?"

He had always been the practical one; she was the dreamer. But, in fact, she had created a plan and had money put aside before she left her job to upgrade the commercial kitchen and set up the processing center—right down to staffing needs. Except now it would need tweaking with the changes Ginny's participation would bring. All that was left to do was pull the trigger.

"I have. Even though it will take a year to get the

commercial space fully operational, I'll start this year with Ginny's support. And in early summer, I'll approach a few stores in town to see if they'd sell my products. Who knows, maybe Maggie would serve them at the diner and offer jars for sale to her customers. We know there's an interest in tourism based on what Gasperini is willing to do to get his hands on land. I'd like to think people would buy jars to take home with them, hence online sales could grow even more with repeat customers."

His eyes were serious as he nodded while she talked. "I'd be happy to look over any vendor contracts and you should have a basic contract for any businesses that accept your product on consignment or straight-up purchase for resale."

This wasn't why she brought up her plans, to get free legal advice. "That's not necessary. I've already discussed it with Rob Adler." She could hear the frosty tone in her voice, and she reined it back. "But thank you."

He didn't seem bothered by her trying to keep him at arm's length for the business. "It's a standing offer and think of it as my way of supporting your company. We can barter. All the apple butter and jam I can eat for a one-hour legal consultation." He traced the curve of her jawline with his finger. "Renee, I'm crazy about you. Just think about it. If I can help in some small way, I'm always as close as a phone. I want to see your business thrive and this is a fantastic concept. You could produce other items to offer, and who knows, maybe you could develop an entire line of beauty products down the road."

That was an interesting idea. "I'd need a chemist for that."

He grabbed his phone. "Okay to tap into your Wi-Fi network?"

She gave him the password and wondered what he was

looking for. It didn't take long before he turned the phone so she could scan the article on the screen.

She was surprised to see there were recipes online for creams, face masks, and more, and all used apples as the main ingredient. She took the phone and her breath caught. Was this a real possibility? "Do you really think I can expand into something like this?"

"With a solid plan and a realistic timeline, you can do anything with the orchard. I know your parents have agreements with some companies to purchase apples, but we live in an area where there is a lot of open space and I'm sure if you needed to expand even more than what you have this year, it's possible to lease land."

"I still have a lot of acreage that isn't planted." She began to make a mental list of things to do, and then as quickly as the ideas began to tumble, she pushed them aside. "I can work on that later; I want to spend the rest of the day focused on us."

He circled the air in front of her face with his hand. "I can tell your wheels are spinning. Get a pad and write down your ideas. You can go back to them later. Keep pushing boundaries and bounce all the ideas you want off me, but first concentrate on the low-hanging fruit."

She laughed. "I see what you did there."

"Jams, jellies, and the apple butter for year one, with the cooking demos. Year two the cookbook and expand into cooking classes and then seriously consider the beauty line. That would make a great year three goal. Make a plan and execute it. You can do this."

Renee liked how he emphasized the word *can*. She moved from her chair to his lap and slid her arms around his neck. Looking deep into his eyes, she could see he was being supportive and that validated her ideas. Not that she needed it from him, but she was glad to have it all the same.

"Change of plans. How about instead of walking around, we stay right here in each other's arms until you have to leave. We can picnic on the porch. After you're back in Dallas, I want to be able to close my eyes and remember what it's like to be here and feel your arms around me."

He nibbled her lips. "You're making it almost impossible to leave."

She longed for time to stop and put a bubble around them. "I'm not trying to but now that we've found each other again, it puts a different spin on time with you. Each minute is precious."

He placed his forehead against hers. "I'm going to miss you like crazy too."

22

*S*ix weeks later, Hank was standing in baggage claim, waiting for his brother and nephew to meet him. They were headed back to the ranch for a surprise visit. No one, not even Renee, knew they were coming home. He shifted his duffel bag from his right to his left hand and withdrew his phone from the back pocket of his Levi's. He was tempted to call Renee but the only thing that stopped him was the off chance she might hear the intercom in the airport. As far as she knew, he was stuck at the office with a trial looming. Which was true but the trial wasn't going to start until the beginning of August and everyone, including him, deserved an early summer vacation.

"Uncle Hank."

He twirled around and dropped to one knee as the little squirt ran full speed in his direction. He scooped Toby up and squeezed him tight.

"Look, Dad, Uncle Hank is right where you said he'd be." The little boy had bleach-blond hair and the same caramel-brown eyes his dad and uncle shared. The Shepard eyes, his mom called them.

"Of course I am. Where did you think I'd be? Halfway to River Junction?"

"Nope." He giggled and swung his small bright-blue backpack around from his back. "Wanna see my new game?"

"Toby." Ford took the backpack. "That's for the plane and maybe the car ride to the ranch. But remember what we talked about; once we get there, we're going to spend most of our time outside with the horses, cows, and doing all kinds of fun stuff."

"I know, like you and Uncle Hank did when you were little like me."

The child's laughter was music to Hank's ears. It had been almost a year since they had spent time together and a lot had happened. But the boy didn't seem to have lost his sparkle. "What do you want to do first, Toby?"

"Dad said I can pick out my very own pony." Toby slipped his arms around Hank's neck. "Did you know Dad can talk to a pony and find out if he's just right?"

Ford flipped Toby a grin. "That's not exactly what I said but I will be able to pick out the best pony for you."

With a quick nod, Toby said, "And I'm gonna name him Dusty."

"That's a very good name but what if you get a girl pony?" Hank asked.

He scrunched up his face and tipped his head. "Dad, can I still name a girl pony Dusty?"

"You betcha." Ford took the boy from Hank and set him on the floor. Clasping Toby's hand Ford said, "Now, we need to get our luggage and then get to the rental car. We still have a couple of hours before we get to the ranch."

Toby wriggled his backpack into place and clasped Hank's hand too.

"Uncle Hank, can we get a snack soon? I'm hungry."

"Whatever you want, Squirt."

He skipped between his dad and uncle. "This is gonna be the bestest vacation ever."

Ford grinned and Hank swore he watched the tension slide away from his brother's shoulders with each step they took toward the conveyor belts overfilled with suitcases and more duffel bags. Toby was right; this was going to be a great vacation.

*H*ank looked at Toby slumped in his booster seat his seat belt, the only thing keeping him upright.

A soft, gentle snore caused Ford to smile. "You never thought a little kid would sound like a bear cub during hibernation, right?"

Hank's gaze flicked from the road to his brother. "Takes after his old man."

"More like his uncle." Ford shook his head. "Ever since we booked our flight, you're all he could jabber on about. Uncle Hank this, Uncle Hank that."

With a chuckle, he said, "What's not to be excited about when you have the best uncle in the world?"

"Too bad he doesn't have the best father." He turned away from Hank and watched the landscape out his window.

"Why do you say that? Toby has the best dad in the world."

With a glance as if to confirm his son was asleep, he said, "Sharon walked out on us, on him. That's going to cause long-term scars. When she first left, he cried in his sleep, calling out 'Mom.' But it's been a few months now and I see his hopeful little face when we pull into the garage, as if he's expecting her car to be there. When it's not, his chin sinks to his little chest and he lets out this huge sigh that would rip your guts out."

Hank's heart constricted as he watched the shutters of hurt and pain drop over Ford's eyes. "I'm sorry. It has to be hard on both of you. But Sharon could have split from you and still had Toby in her life. Most divorced couples share custody. She used the split as an excuse to not be a mother. That's on her, not you."

Ford tapped his temple. "I know that here but how do you get a kid to understand that you're gonna show up and not leave him, no matter what?"

"One day at a time. And I think coming out to the ranch will be good for both of you."

Ford pressed his fingers into his eyes. With a catch in his voice, he said, "I'm glad you pushed the idea and didn't give up on me. It's hard going back home as the screwup son."

Tightening his grip on the wheel, he said, "You need to put the blame where it lies and that's not entirely on your shoulders. Yes, you played a role in your marriage falling apart. It takes two but give yourself credit. You show up every day for Toby, going to work, being around for homework and meals. That's what he needs. Consistency. Stability."

"Yeah, work has been really good about my flex schedule and if I have to be at the rehab clinic on the weekend, I can take Toby with me. He hangs out in the office at the clinic."

"That's good. How's work going?"

"It's my dream job, working with horses every day, getting them to recover from all kinds of injuries. It's what I always wanted to do."

"Good to hear." Hank fell silent the closer they got to the ranch. He planned on spending a little time at the house with the family before he was going to saddle Ranger and head over to the orchard.

"How's the love life, big brother?"

"It's fine. Renee and I have been talking most nights but this is the first time I've been able to get back home—and with her construction plans underway converting the barn into the store, she hasn't been able to take a break either."

"I hope she likes your surprise."

He slowed the car as he exited from the highway. "I plan on spending a lot of time with you and Toby too. I've missed your ugly face and his cute one."

"And I can't wait to chow down on Mom's chocolate cake and whatever else she wants to whip up. Oh, and did you say the annual Shepard BBQ is this weekend? Is Renee planning on going?"

"You know Mom would never take no for an answer so I expect she'll be there and now it will be with me."

"I like that look on your face."

Hank felt the wrinkles on his brow deepen. "What are you talking about?"

"When you talk about her, everything in your demeanor changes. It's like you can finally take a deep breath or something." He pointed out the windshield. "Look, there's the sign for the Filler Up Diner. That's another thing I want to do while I'm home, take Toby in for a milkshake."

He liked how Ford didn't dwell on his outward appearance and moved on to milkshakes. But his brother was right. Renee played a huge part in how he felt, but it was coming home to River Junction that felt good too. He drove slowly down Main Street, past The Trading Post, the diner, The Lucky Bucket, and Robert Adler's office. There was still a welcome sign hanging over the porch steps. At least he was around to help the townsfolk with the Gasperini issue. As they left town, Hank pressed down on the gas pedal. He needed to get back to the ranch, sweep his mom into a bear hug, and then find his lady and kiss her breathless.

. . .

*F*ord unbuckled his seat belt as Hank slowed down and came to a stop at the gates of the Stone's Throw Ranch. "Hey, buddy, it's time to wake up. We're almost at Gram and Gramps' house."

"What?" He rubbed his eyes and then popped his seat belt. "Dad. Look out there. Cows." In the distance, part of the herd was grazing. "Where are the horses and the real cowboys?"

"Toby, did you know your dad is a real cowboy too?"

The child's eyes widened. "Really, Dad?"

"A long time ago, Uncle Hank and I worked on this very ranch riding horses every day, taking care of the cows and being good stewards to the land."

He screwed up his face. "Who's Stewart?"

Ford held out his hands. "Why don't you sit in my lap; that way as soon as we get to the house, you can surprise your grandparents."

He quickly swung one foot and then the other in between the bucket seats and perched on Ford's lap. He was almost bouncing with excitement. "Come on, Uncle Hank, we gotta get going. Gram is gonna be so happy to see me. It's been almost a whole year."

Hank chuckled. "You were here for Christmas, remember? But it does seem like a lifetime ago."

The smile that had shone so bright on his face dimmed as he looked at his shoes. "Can I call Mommy tonight?"

Wrapping his arms around his son, Ford said, "Yes. We'll make sure to call her before dinner."

Hank jumped in, "And you can tell her all about your new pony too."

Toby brightened a little and nodded his head. "Okay, Uncle Hank."

They made the remainder of the trip full of I spy on the half mile road. Hank drove slowly to give his nephew a chance to see it all and he wanted to take it in as well. With a look at Ford, he felt the excitement too.

The moment the car came to a stop and the engine was off, Toby pushed open the door and raced toward the kitchen. He didn't slow down until he turned the knob and looked back to see if Ford and Hank were right behind him.

"Come on. Quick. I wanna hear Gram say, *the Shepard boys have come home.* You know she says that every time she sees us."

As the men reached the top step, the door swung open and their mom stood there. Her hand flew to her chest. "Be still my heart. Do my eyes deceive me? Henry, come quick, the Shepard boys are home, all three of them."

She bent down and flung her arms around Toby while she looked at Ford and Hank. "This is such a wonderful surprise. Why didn't you tell us you were coming and how long are you staying and what do you want for dinner and well"—she took a ragged breath—"I just can't believe you're really standing on our back porch."

"Hey, Mom." Hank stepped closer and bussed her cheek. "Dad inside?"

"He just came in for lunch."

Toby wriggled from her arms and dashed inside the house, calling out to his grandfather.

She stood and opened her arms wide. Hank and Ford stepped into her embrace. "My boys are here."

"Surprise, Mom," Hank said. "And we're staying for two weeks."

She blinked. "Is that all? Well, I'm going to have to see if I can convince you to stay a little longer. That won't be nearly enough time to spend with Toby on top of getting ready for the barbeque this weekend."

"Now, Maeve, the boys just got here and you're already thinking about them leaving." His dad held on to Toby's hand and grinned. "It's good to have you home." He looked from Hank to Ford. "Both of you." He held the door wide. "Instead of standing in the doorway, how about you come inside and tell us what prompted this visit. Not that I am objecting. I'm just wondering if you can use the reason to come back more often."

Hank said, "I'll get our bags and be right in." He waited until his family was out of sight before he took a deep breath, slowly inhaling the fresh Montana air through his nose and out through his mouth. Looking at his parents with Toby and hearing his mother already conspiring to find ways to convince them to stay longer, and of course his dad tossing in his two cents was a gut punch. They were all getting older and life had a way of changing on a dime. He knew one thing: while he was here, he needed to get his priorities straight before it was too late.

"Son." His dad's voice cut through his train of thought. "Everything okay out here?"

He didn't turn around and cleared the lump from his throat. "Yeah, Pop. Just taking a moment but I'll be right there."

23

*R*enee made her way to the field where the new nursery stock had been planted. As she walked the rows, she was pleased to see semi-dwarf trees were thriving. This was the future of her orchard and it certainly looked promising. She wandered to the edge of the river and let the sounds of the gurgling water sluicing over rocks and around flood-made berms add to her sense of calm. The only thing that would have made this moment more perfect was if Hank was standing next to her. She exhaled and tipped back her head, letting the afternoon sun caress her face. The sound of hooves drawing closer pulled her from a meditative state.

Coming from the Stone's Throw Ranch was a rider galloping. Fear snaked around her heart. Could something be wrong with Henry or Maeve and someone was coming to get her?

As the distance lessened, there was something about the cowboy in the saddle—and for a split second her heart quickened. Hank.

But then her shoulders sagged. He wasn't going to be

coming back to River Junction until the fall or maybe until Thanksgiving.

A breeze kicked up, whipping her long hair across her face and as she pulled it back, the cowboy's hat flipped off his head. He didn't slow his pace, lifting his hand in greeting.

"Hank." His name slipped out on a whisper and her heart raced. He bent low over the horse's neck and urged him forward, easily clearing the fence and coming to a halt on the riverbank.

He slipped from the saddle and looped the reins over the fence rail before hopping into the water that separated them. She was at a loss for words as he wrapped his arms around her and pulled her into a searing kiss.

When he loosened his embrace, she looked into his eyes. "What are you doing here?"

"Surprising you."

She cupped his cheek with her hand. "You look tired. Did you just get here?"

"I've been home a couple of hours—time to see the folks and spend a little quality time with Toby and Ford. Toby got his first pony today so I stuck around for a bit while he did a few laps in the paddock, and then Ranger and I got over here as quick as we could."

It didn't matter that he hadn't come here first; Renee was thrilled to be in his arms.

He searched her eyes. "Are you happy to see me?"

"Beyond happy." The world faded away as they eased to the soft grass. How long they stayed there was lost on her. All that mattered was he was here now.

Ranger nickered softly and Hank said, "I should get him back to the barn. Come for dinner tonight. You know there's plenty."

Renee said, "It's family time and if you want, we can have dinner tomorrow night."

His brow wrinkled and the lines between his eyes creased. "You are family."

She gave him a light kiss. "You haven't seen Ford and Toby in a long time. Be with them and we'll have time together tomorrow, and I can guarantee we'll make the most of every minute you're here. Which I didn't ask, but when do you have to leave?"

"Trying to get rid of me already?" He brushed a wayward lock from her face. The look in his eyes was tender.

"Not at all. I'm just trying to figure out how many days I have to pack everything in. We have adventures to take, maybe a hike, stargazing, picnics, fishing—you know, stuff."

"Don't forget the annual Shepard barbeque on Saturday. I'm hoping you—and Ginny too—will come. Mom's cooking up a storm and as an added incentive, they hired a pit master to cook the meat. Not sure who it is but from what my dad says, he's one of the best."

"Can I think about it?"

He pulled her up and slipped his arm around her waist. "You have until Friday to decide. After that I'm going to let Mom know that she needs to pick you up."

With a laugh, she said, "Just a little mom guilt tossed in, I'll say yes."

His brown eyes grew serious. "I don't want to miss a moment of time that we can be together."

She gave a thoughtful sigh. "How can I say no to that handsome face? And as long as you're sure it's okay with your family, I'll extend the invite to Ginny as well."

"Good, now about dinner tonight? Ford would love to see you and I want you to meet Toby. He's a great kid."

Her heart once again tightened when she thought of that little boy whose mom walked out and left him. Having people around might be helpful for everyone. "I'll come on the condition that I bring something for dinner."

He picked her up and twirled her around while she laughed, then he said, "I'll pick you up at five."

*J*ust before Hank was due to arrive, Renee was sitting in the living room looking over the estimate for the new appliances. It would stretch her budget, but Ginny had given her input into what she thought would be best and given that she was the chef, Renee would follow her suggestions. Her cell rang and she answered it on speakerphone.

"Hey, Ginny, where are you? I thought you'd be home hours ago."

"That's why I'm calling. Any chance you could come and get me? I've had a small accident."

She leaped up from the couch. "Where are you? Are you alright?"

"In the River Junction emergency room. But I hit my head, and the sheriff wanted me to get checked out, and if that wasn't enough, my car's been towed someplace to get fixed."

"Sit tight. I'm on my way." A shiver raced down her spine. Ginny had a way of underplaying everything, so if she had hit her head, there was sure to be a concern about a concussion. She grabbed her handbag and keys and flung open the kitchen door to find Hank, with his fist eye height, ready to knock.

He grinned. "Anxious to have dinner with the family?"

"I have to go. Ginny's been in a car accident."

The smile faded and he held out his hand. "I'll drive."

She closed and locked the door. As they crossed the porch, she said, "You have dinner with your family."

"I'll call Mom and let her know we can't make it. She'll

understand." He pulled open the passenger door to his rental car and waited until she was inside before he closed it and jogged around the front. As the engine purred, he asked, "Where is she?"

"At the ER. I didn't ask what happened, but she said the sheriff insisted she get checked out. Oh, and she said her car was headed to a shop to get repaired."

He clasped her hand. The warmth wrapped around her heart like a cozy blanket. Not that she wasn't still freaked out knowing Ginny was hurt. How could this have happened? She drove like an old lady, slow and extra cautious.

The drive into town seemed to take twice as long as normal. Renee had her phone clutched in her free hand while Hank still held the other. They had never been in a situation like this when they were dating. She was pleasantly surprised to see he was as solid as the mountain range. With a glance or two at his profile, she noted he kept his eyes on the road ahead.

"She didn't say what had happened."

With a slow shake of her head, Renee said, "No. I was too freaked out to ask, and she sounded okay. Once I see her, I'll feel better."

His cell rang, and she grew quiet as he answered on speakerphone.

"Hey, Mom. I was going to call you. Renee can hear you too."

"Hank, is everything okay? I expected you and Renee to be here by now."

"Sorry. Renee's friend Ginny had a car accident and is at the ER in River Junction. We're headed there now to pick her up, so we'll miss supper."

"I hope she's okay. And you do what needs to be done. Will you be going back to Renee's after?"

He glanced her way. "Yeah, apparently the sheriff

insisted she get checked. I know Renee won't want to leave her when we get back to the house."

"That's fine. How about I send over enough dinner for the three of you? Ford can slip a few casserole dishes into her oven. This way, it will be waiting for you."

Renee leaned closer to the phone. "That's not necessary, Maeve."

A soft laugh emanated from the phone. "Ree, please let me do this. I've cooked enough food for a small army, also known as my boys. In fact, you'll be helping me not have as many leftovers."

Hank shrugged his shoulders and grinned. He mouthed, *you're not going to win this battle.*

"The key is under the mat. But have dinner first. I think we'll be at the clinic a while."

"Mom, don't forget dessert. I'm counting on a piece of strawberry shortcake."

She tugged on his hand. "Stop. Whatever she sends will be more than enough and don't forget I made dessert too."

He winked at her. "Anyway, thanks, Mom—and I'll give you a call later."

Renee said, "Yes, thank you, Maeve. I can speak for Ginny, and she says thank you too. The only thing I make that she likes is coffee and toast."

"Drive safely, and if Ginny needs anything, be sure to let me know. Bye now." She disconnected the call.

Hank clicked on his blinker and pulled into the large parking area at the emergency room. "Having a hot meal waiting for when we get back will be nice. You can get Ginny comfortable and I'll plate up dinner."

She blinked a couple of times. "When did you morph into this new man sitting next to me?"

A flash of surprise flitted through his eyes. "Renee, I haven't changed that much since we were kids. I know you might think I'm selfish for some of my life choices, but when it comes to the people I care about, I'd walk through hell and back to help."

She looked away and then back. "I didn't mean anything negative."

Softly, he said, "I'm sure you think my life has been perfect. But it's hard living so far away from my family. Sometimes, as adults, we make certain choices for the right reasons that leave us with the life we thought we wanted."

A vise tightened around her heart. She had taken a potshot at him, and he didn't deserve it. He was the one who had driven her to town and changed plans with his family to help her and Ginny. If there were lingering hard feelings she needed to discuss them with him—but now wasn't the time to do it. In this moment, the only person who was important was Ginny. "I'm sorry. That was unfair. Can we talk about this another time?"

He lifted their clasped hands and kissed the underside of her wrist. "We can and should." He pulled the key from the ignition and opened his door. "I love you, Renee, and I know that you love me too even if you're not ready to say it. We have plenty of time to sort through any lingering hurts from the past as long as we don't let the past color our future."

"Hank? You, you love me?"

He placed his fingers lightly over her mouth. "I do and we're fine. I'm a big boy and I'll be able to handle the conversation when the time is right."

She leaned across the console and placed her hand on his cheek before kissing his mouth, savoring the sweet connection between them. "We carried a lot of hurt for a long time. But I do love you with all my heart. I gave it to you a long time ago and no matter what I said out of anger, it's always been and always will be you."

He looked deep into her eyes, causing her insides to act

like a can of jumping beans. "It's the same for me." He nodded in the direction of the door. "We should get inside."

"We should but I'm glad we took these couple of moments for me to say what was on my heart."

"I want you to always be completely honest with me. We're lucky we have a second chance at love."

She kissed him again. "Very lucky."

24

*T*he next ten days evaporated for Hank like an early morning mist over the valley. He had spent a lot of time with Toby and Ford while Renee worked.

A couple of times, she skipped out early, and they all went for a trail ride.

At first, Toby had been cautious around her. More than likely because of his mother abandoning him, but in less than two days, he was chattering like they were old friends.

Now Hank had three days left, and he wanted to have a very special night with Renee, but darned if he knew what to do. Slipping away for a night wasn't an option. She was under the gun with the new kitchen project at the orchard.

Out of all their old friends, Maggie was the most romantic. She would have some great ideas.

He hurried to the stairs and found his mom in the kitchen stirring up what he hoped were her cowboy cookies. Giving her a peck on the cheek, he said, "I'm going into town. Do you need anything?"

With a wide smile, she said, "No. Will you and Renee be here for dinner tonight?"

"I hope not." He saw her smile dip. "Sorry, that's not

how I meant for it to come out. I'm planning a very special evening with her, just the two of us. But can I ask a favor? Can you make a nice dinner for Saturday night? I'm leaving on Sunday, and I'd really like it if we could get together, and Ginny too?"

She patted his cheek in her motherly way. "I was already planning on it. Is there something special you'd like?"

"Just toss something on the grill. It doesn't have to be fancy. Just being with the people I love is all I want."

"Should I call Renee or will you ask her and Ginny?"

"I'll take care of it." He kissed her cheek. "See you later."

"Drive safely."

If his mom had anything else to say, her words were cut off by the kitchen door slamming behind him. He glanced in the direction of the paddock.

Ford perched on the top slat of the fence, watching Toby trot Dusty around. By the slope of his brother's shoulders, it was easy to see he had finally relaxed. He even extended his vacation for an extra week. He said Toby was having a blast, and when they got back to Tennessee, he'd be with a babysitter all day.

He and Ford agreed kids were meant to be outside, not stuck in a condo.

Hank lifted a hand in greeting before he got into the truck, and Ford returned the gesture. Now he was off to Maggie's.

Hank parked his truck on Main Street just down the road from the entrance to the Filler Up. He waited half a minute before getting out. Rob Adler was sitting on the top porch step to his law office. It was easy to notice his shoulders were slumped as if the weight of the world had settled on them.

Hank looked both ways and jogged across the street,

stopping at the bottom of the steps. "Hey, Rob, how's it going today?"

He gave a half-hearted smile. "It's going." He tipped his head and squinted his eyes. "When are you headed back to Dallas?"

"Sunday."

"Huh." He slid over and pointed to the space next to him. "Got time to chat?"

With a quick glance at his watch, Hank sat down. "I do."

A van crept by with school-age kids, headed out of town. "Is the summer camp still in session out near Coyote Ridge?"

"A couple more weeks and the kiddos will be headed back to school."

"Ford and I went there for a couple of summers. That was before we started working on the ranch. I think Mom liked it since we burned off all the energy before we got home."

Rob gave a snort. "You boys were a handful. Is Ford's son a chip off the old block?"

"He has a lot of energy, but Ford's a good dad. Being at the ranch has been good for both of them."

Rob gave him a side-look. "And you? Can't wait to get back to the city?"

Hank looked down the street and then up. "A few years ago, I would have answered the question very differently than today." He clasped his hands together and leaned forward. "When I got the phone call that Dad was hurt, it was like a switch I unknowingly had inside of me flipped. Waiting for that flight was the longest night of my life."

"What about Renee Mitchell? The talk around town is the two of you have reconnected."

"True statement."

He turned on the step so he faced Hank. "This might be

presumptuous of me, but have you talked about what you're going to do long term?"

"We're doing a long-distance relationship."

"Are you looking forward to cozying up to a phone this winter?"

Wow. Rob didn't pull any punches. Not that it was his business, but no one else had talked to him about his romance with Renee. "No. But I have a career in Dallas. I'm going to try and get back as often as I can."

"Hank, that's not a relationship; it's a romance of convenience for you. Have you thought about what you want your future to look like? Have you considered all the factors—your parents, the ranch, Renee's growing business, and your career?"

"It's all I can think about. When I went back to Dallas, to my sterile apartment, the loneliness engulfed me. The one thing that kept me going were my conversations with Renee. I couldn't wait to get back here. So I called Ford and hatched a plan to surprise everyone."

"You needed Ford to surprise Renee?" The older man's brows knitted together as he waited for Hank to continue.

"I was hoping Ford would get here and realize this is the best place to raise Toby, around people who love them and on the ranch."

He nodded his head. "What has Ford decided?"

Where was Rob going with this conversation? If he wanted to know about Ford, maybe he should take a ride out to the ranch. "He's extended his trip by a week, so yeah, I think he's contemplating a change. He could easily take over the day-to-day operations of the ranch and even have a consulting business for horses. He's like some kind of horse whisperer."

"So I've heard." He grinned. "Now that you've formulated a plan for your brother, what is stopping you from doing the same?"

Hank dropped his head and looked at Rob. "You're a pretty good attorney, aren't you?"

"I get by, but you didn't answer the question." Now his hazel eyes twinkled. "Here is what I think you should do. Part of this is definitely selfish, and the other side of it, well, it's what you really want, so I'm going to give you permission."

"Is this your closing argument?"

With a clap on Hank's shoulder, he said, "Or my opening for you to stew on it." He cleared his throat. "Renee is expanding her business so for her to relocate to Dallas—or anywhere for that matter—is impossible. And I have known since you two were youngsters following each other around town that she is the only girl for you."

"I—"

Rob cut him off. "Hold on. I also happen to know of a thriving law practice that is looking to take on a brilliant young attorney who could be just what this growing town needs. Especially with this developer sniffing around and any other trouble the winds from the west might blow in." He stood. "Hank, I want you to seriously consider buying my practice. I'd like to stay on, part-time only, for a year or two while I plan my next steps. Take all the time you need to make the best decision for you and the town." It was then Hank heard the catch in the older man's voice as he said, "You are the only person I'd trust to carry on."

Rob strode into the building and the door closed with a thud. Hank sat on the step, mildly stunned. Not only was there an offer on the table, but based on the conversation he'd had with Rob a few months ago, there was a lot that happened in a small-town lawyer's office. He wouldn't be bored, but was he ready to leave the partnership behind and move home? His folks weren't getting any younger; Ford might just move Toby here if there was a wider family support system, and of course, Renee. Were they ready to be in each other's lives on a regular basis or did the long-distance relationship suit her?

His head spun with questions and he hated when he didn't already know the answers for what to do with his life. Could it have been fate that Rob was sitting on the steps at the same time he drove into town? The longer he sat here, the more questions filled his thoughts. However, the most important question for this moment was planning a date that would show Renee just how much he loved her. He pushed himself up from the steps and ambled down the walkway, turning to look at the two-story building that housed the law office and who knew what else. Maybe an apartment if he was fortunate. If this was a move he would make, he wanted to have a place of his own. Staying at the ranch for a vacation was one thing, and he and Renee weren't ready to live together. Not yet.

Hank moseyed down the sidewalk and really looked at the town. It was thriving. Some people he recognized, others were new to him, but everyone was friendly. He pulled open the heavy glass door and entered the diner. The aroma of fresh coffee permeated the air and he took a seat at the counter. Maggie nodded in his direction as she delivered plates of food to a couple.

When she got to the counter, she said, "Hank, this is a surprise. Coffee?"

"Please and what's the muffin of the day?"

"I have three. Corn, coffee cake, or blueberry."

"I'll take a blueberry grilled with butter, please."

"Coming right up." She clipped a ticket to the spinner and gave it a whirl for Mack to grab. Leaning against the counter, she asked, "What brings you to town this morning? I figure with just a few days left, you'd want to spend them all with Renee."

He smiled, knowing that Maggie knew his comings and goings. "I do but I need your help." He gave her a conspiratorial wink. "I want to plan a date that will knock her socks off."

"Honey, just showing up is all she needs, and spend time with her. But if you're looking for something special and asking for my help, enjoy your coffee while I think about how a handsome guy could woo me."

He chuckled. Woo. There was a quaint word for a date with the love of his life. He held up his cup in a salute. "Thanks, Mags."

25

*R*enee scuffed her feet as she crossed the gravel drive at a turtle's pace. In a few days, Hank would be gone and their romance would consist of phone calls, emails, and text messages. Again. It was hard for them both to live for tiny snippets of time, but as long as they both were committed, it could work. *Besides, I'm not about to walk away from the orchard or the man.* As much as she loved Hank, the one thing she had learned over the years was that she would follow her heart.

A toot of a horn caused her to look up. A dark sedan eased to a stop. Her heart sank. Another go-round with that horrid Gasperini? She straightened her spine, prepared to do battle if necessary.

The driver got out and walked to the back of the car, withdrawing two shopping bags.

"Can I help you?"

"Special delivery for Renee Mitchell." He held out the bags with a smile. "There's a note inside one of the bags and I've been asked to wait for you."

She looked down at her dirt-streaked clothes. "I can't go anywhere right now. I just got done working."

"I was told you might protest so please read the note and I'll be waiting whenever you're ready."

Cautiously, she took the bags and hurried to the porch to find this note that was supposed to explain what was going on. Resting on something wrapped in tissue paper was a large white envelope with her name printed across the front. She eased the card out. It was an invitation.

I hope you're ready for a night you'll always remember. Please wear the outfit in the bags and when you're ready, Mason, aka the driver, will bring you to where I will be waiting. See you very soon, my love. H.

Her heart raced as she pulled each item from the bag and when they were all on the porch swing, she unwrapped each one. There was a long overshirt, boho-style sleeveless floral sundress, and brown ankle booties.

Ginny opened the kitchen door. "What are you doing out here?"

She held up the dress. "Hank sent these and a driver for me." Her hand flew to her mouth. "Do you think he's going to propose to me tonight?"

"By the looks of all the trouble he went to, he wants it to be a night you'll remember." She grabbed Renee's hand and pulled her into the kitchen. "You need to get showered and I'll steam the dress for you." She gave her a playful shove in the direction of the stairs. "Go on now and don't forget lipstick. Not that the man needs to be reminded, but you want them to look kissably irresistible."

Renee could hear the nerves in her giggle. "That's not even a word."

"It is now." She pointed to the stairs again. "Get going. You don't want to keep that man waiting."

. . .

*R*enee came downstairs wearing the freshly steamed dress. She had pulled her hair into a clip so the waves cascaded down her back. And as Ginny had suggested, her makeup was done and flawless, at least based on the amount of time she had spent. It seemed as if her feet didn't touch the floor as she walked into the kitchen. With a low whistle, Ginny gave her a grin of approval.

"That man knows how to pick out the perfect outfit." She twirled her finger around, indicating Renee should do a spin.

"Do I look okay?"

Ginny gave her a hug. "Beautiful is the only word that springs to mind. And if you want to share any good news when you get home, just tap on my door."

Renee pressed a hand to her tummy. "Why am I so nervous?"

"It's not every day that a guy goes to this much trouble for his woman. Now, don't keep the man waiting." She kissed her cheek. "Have a wonderful night."

"Thank you and find a scary book to read so you'll still be awake when I get home."

Ginny laughed and opened the kitchen door. "Not to worry, I'll be all ears."

Renee's fingers tingled and she took several deep breaths to keep the blood circulating. Fainting was not an option, not that she knew what it felt like to faint, but she didn't need to find out now.

Mason held the car door for her and she slid into the back seat. "Thank you."

"You're welcome, Renee. Now sit back and relax. We'll be at your destination in approximately sixty minutes."

She felt her eyes widen. What the heck was Hank doing? Easing back into the deep, comfy cushions, she relaxed as the car sped down the highway in the direction of the mountains.

After an hour or so the car slowed, turned right, and bumped over the gravel road. They drew closer to a small cabin. A ribbon of smoke curled from the chimney and Hank stood on the porch.

Mason parked the vehicle and hurriedly opened her door, extending his hand to her.

She took it. Hank was by her side, snaking an arm around her waist and pulling her close, claiming her mouth with his.

"I'm so happy to see you." He said thank you to Mason who got back in the car before heading in the direction they had come. "Welcome to Serenity Cabin." He swept his arm around all that encompassed the log cabin and the expanse of the mountain range behind it. "What do you think?"

Placing her hand over her thudding heart, she took a deep breath, "It's just beautiful here. Who does it belong to?"

"Us. I discovered this gem and thought we could use a hideaway when I'm in town. It's furnished but you can decorate it any way you want." He kissed her cheek.

Ginny had been right. Tonight, her life would change. At some point during the evening, Hank was going to propose. "Can we go in? I'd love a tour."

"Come with me." He took her hand and they strolled up the wide wooden plank steps. A porch swing swayed gently in the breeze and she couldn't help but stop to savor the stunning views. The mountain peaks were dotted white with patches of snow. In a couple of hours, the sun would be setting. "Can we sit on the porch to watch the stars?"

He nuzzled her neck. "If that's what you'd like, yes. Grand tour and then we can have dinner."

He eased the door open and she took a step inside. The first floor was an open floor plan with a massive fireplace dominating the back side with an oversized sofa in front of it. There was a small kitchen tucked into a corner and a square pine table set complete with glowing candles and china. A bottle of wine was in a chiller bucket.

"You did all of this today?"

He lifted her hand to his lips and kissed the underside of her wrist. "I had help. Maggie took care of the food and wine, and I raided Mom's china cabinet for candles and dishes."

Renee strolled around the room, her fingertips grazing the tops of tables until she stood near the fireplace. She brushed the dampness from her cheeks. "I'm shocked."

He held up his finger. "Hold that thought." In a few long strides, he uncorked the wine and poured two glasses before reaching her side. He clinked his glass to hers. "To us. And our future."

She took a sip of the crisp, cool wine. "This is delicious. Shall we sit down? The sofa looks pretty cozy."

"I like how you think." He sat and pulled her onto his lap. Cupping her cheek with his hand, he lowered his lips to hers. "I've been thinking about this moment all day."

A flutter of nerves caused her stomach to flip. "I wasn't expecting all of this." She looked around the room and down at her outfit. "Thank you for the dress and shoes, but why did you send them?"

"I wanted to do something nice for you; in fact, I'm wearing new clothes too. It's as if we're starting over fresh with nothing from the past hanging over our relationship."

She laughed softly. "The past is what made us who we are today. It's nothing we should run away from."

"I am definitely not running away, but I'm ready to embrace our future. So, I have a question to ask you."

It was a good thing she had only sipped a bit of wine the way her nerves were prodding her insides. "The cabin wasn't a big enough surprise?"

"This cabin can be where we meet when I come home so that we can have privacy. I love being with you. It's not that I don't enjoy being with our family and friends, but we need our time too."

"Are you suggesting we start living out here?"

"No." The crease between his eyes deepened. "This is our hideaway. You live at the orchard and when I come to town, we have a place we can be together."

Renee eased off his lap and went back to stand by the fireplace. "You're not moving to River Junction?"

"What gave you that idea?"

It hit her like a ton of bricks. The surprise was the cabin, not a proposal for marriage. He planned a romantic evening where they could be alone and enjoy each other's company. Her chin trembled and a lump lodged in her throat. "What else did you want to ask me?"

"If you'd spend Thanksgiving with me in Dallas? It will be great. I thought we could do a turkey trot, and then I could get tickets for the football game. The Cowboys are playing at home this year and after the game, we'll get all dressed up if you want and have a late dinner."

"My parents are coming to Montana for Thanksgiving. Spending it in Dallas isn't possible, at least not this year. Plans have been made and I'm looking forward to showing the orchard off to them. They've only heard me talk about the changes." She drained her wineglass and walked to the table for a refill. Tears threatened to leak from her eyes if she couldn't find a way to stop them. Maybe if she said she was hungry they could have dinner and get this night over with. There was no way she was about to tell Hank she thought he was going to ask her to be his bride. That dream was either still on hold or completely crushed.

"Renee." He slipped his arms around her and pulled her to his chest. "I'm sorry. I shouldn't have sprung that on you. I got carried away thinking we could have a romantic long weekend in Dallas."

With an audible sigh, she patted his hand. "Family time is very important to me and as the only child, I love spending every holiday I can with my parents. While I lived in Chicago, I never missed a major holiday."

He kissed her temple. "We'll do it some other time. There is always something going on in that city." He eased her around and his smile morphed into concern. "Hey, why the tears?"

Despite her best effort, those darn things were sliding down her cheeks at an alarming rate. "It's no big deal." She shrugged her shoulders. "I'm fine."

"Renee, something has upset you. Tell me."

She placed her glass on the table and took a step from his arms. She needed to be honest with him and not bottle up how she felt. That mistake wasn't about to be replayed. "I thought when you went to so much trouble for tonight that you were going to propose to me."

Hank took a step back; his mouth went slack-jawed and his eyes grew round. "What? Like down on one knee?"

His reaction was not what she had expected. "Never mind. It was a stupid idea. Forget about it."

He reached for her hand and she brushed it away.

"Really. It's fine. It's just that you made such a big deal out of this, with a driver, a new outfit; it was quite the buildup. I think the cabin is charming and you're right, we'll enjoy spending time here when you come back."

She lifted a lid on a platter and discovered it held chicken piccata, one of her favorite dishes. And if Maggie made it, the flavor should dance on her tongue, but tonight it would be like sawdust. "We should enjoy this delicious dinner while it's still warm."

"Renee," Hank stammered, "I am so sorry. I didn't know you were there, like ideas of marriage already."

"No worries. Really. It was just me jumping to an incorrect conclusion." She crossed the short space between him and pecked his lips. Looking deep into his eyes, she smiled. "Really. Now we should eat. I'm ravenous."

She tugged on his hand and he pulled out a chair for her. The air between them was charged with unspoken emotions from them both.

How was she going to get them back to an easygoing banter? "How are Toby and Dusty getting along?" She snapped the linen napkin open and placed it over her lap, carefully avoiding his eyes.

"Ford extended their visit by a week but he's going to have a tough time separating Toby from his mount."

"A true cowboy." She filled her plate while passing serving dishes to Hank. Just as she suspected, everything was tasteless. The only thing she could do was get through dinner, watch a few stars come out, and then beg off with a headache so Hank would take her home. With a forced smile, she finally looked him in the eyes. "Hopefully they'll be able to come back soon. From what I've seen, this trip has been good for everyone in the Shepard family."

He placed his hand over hers. "Renee, please don't be upset with me."

And she knew she wasn't upset with him, but she was with herself. She leaned across the table, letting her lips linger on his. "I promise you, I'm not." She kissed him again. "And you know I would never lie to you about something like this, not even to spare your feelings."

His shoulders leveled out and he flashed that charming grin that made her heart melt every time. "I love you with all my heart and spending time with you again have been the best days of my adult life."

She cupped his cheek even as her heart sank. "Mine too."

---

26

*H*ank replayed that night at the cabin again as his boot-clad feet were propped on the over-sized mahogany desk. He yanked on his tie and unbuttoned the first two buttons on his shirt. It had been a brutal day. His vacation to River Junction had only been a month ago. He missed the steady pace of ranch life but even more, he was lost without Renee. The quick texts, phone calls, and video chats helped them get back on solid ground after their misunderstanding about the future, but technology was a poor substitute for face-to-face. He kept wondering what he was doing in Dallas when the woman he loved was fifteen hundred miles away.

His cell buzzed with an incoming call. It was his mom's ringtone. "Hey, Mom." He plowed ahead without waiting for her to speak. "Is everything okay at the house?"

"It is. I just wanted to check on my oldest son to see how you were doing, being back in the big city and all."

He looked out the window. The view was spectacular from the tenth floor and his office building was on the outskirts of the city so it overlooked the crowded suburbs.

On the streets below, cars were doing the stop-and-go dance during the end-of-the-day rush to get home.

"It's business as usual." But it wasn't at all like it had been six months ago before he went back to Montana and reconnected with Renee. In the last few days, he realized he was a fool. Not the success he enjoyed in his professional life but in all the ways that really mattered.

"You have that distant tone in your voice again. I was hoping coming home would have pushed that into the past."

His mom's voice wasn't harsh; she was just stating a fact. He wanted to unburden himself to her, but her advice would be to follow his heart, pack his bags, and make the long drive home. A part of him wanted to do just that but doubts lingered.

"Hank, do you want to talk about what's weighing heavy on your heart?"

And just like that, she'd cut to the core of his problem. "It's okay. I've had a long day, that's all." Anxious to change the subject, he asked, "How's Dad doing?"

"Happy to be working but missing Toby. That little boy sure did brighten our little slice of heaven."

"Dad's not working too hard, is he?" His father was a stubborn man but not foolhardy.

"He's not riding as much, instead zipping around in the UTV. I think long hours in the saddle cause some discomfort. Not that he'd say a word. I haven't seen him this happy in a long time and he still gets to keep track of every cowboy, horse, and the cattle."

He sighed. "Driving the UTV is a good compromise. I wouldn't want him to slide backward."

"He modified his workday even if it pained him to do so. He's not a young man anymore."

A sliver of concern snaked down his back. Neither he

nor his brother were there to keep a handle on the ranch. Maybe that too was a mistake.

"Have you heard from Ford recently?"

"A couple of days ago. He's having trouble with Sharon again. Toby asks for his momma, and she still won't call the boy. What kind of mother does that?"

Living in Tennessee couldn't be easy, but like everyone, Ford needed to find his own path. "That's rough, but he'll figure out what he needs to do. I'll give him a call and see if they want to come home for the holidays. Toby can miss preschool and Ford gets a couple weeks' holiday time at the end of the year so an extended stay might be just what they need."

"Does that mean you're coming home too?"

The hopeful tone in her voice constricted his heart. He had spent too many years working through the holidays so other lawyers with kids could have extra time off, but his family had suffered.

"I plan on being home and a few long weekends before then."

His mom grew quiet.

"Mom, are you okay if I come home more?" He heard her sniff and he felt like a jerk; he hadn't meant to make her cry.

"The door is always open and the coffee's always on."

A smile spread across his face. He wished he was walking in the old kitchen door right now. "Momma, have I told you lately that you're the best mother for me?"

"I've had some experience. Since I've just gotten a huge kudos, I have to ask, what's going on with you and Renee? I saw her at the post office the other day and she was looking down in the mouth."

That didn't make him feel good to know she was sad. It was just one more reason to really think about what he was going to do next. "Mom, do me a favor. Ask her to come for dinner on Sunday. All she does is work and I'm pretty sure she couldn't say no to some of your home cooking. Maybe even mention you'll make that chocolate cake she loves so much."

"I'll call her tomorrow and let you know what she says."

An idea was beginning to gel. "Don't tell her I suggested it, and let me know what time you're eating so I can call and video chat with you all."

After he said goodbye to his mom, he drafted a letter to his boss and sent it via email. Next, he pulled up his caseload and prioritized what he needed to finish up before he left for the day. Sunday was in six days away and he had a lot to wrap up. Who says a lawyer can't have an impulsive streak?

$\mathcal{L}$ife was a whirlwind of activity over the next four days. Hank had no idea how he had pulled it off, but the back of his SUV was packed with boxes. He was finally in the driver's seat and driving north on the open road. In the predawn light, the orange sun promised the day to be another scorcher. He had a cooler on the passenger seat, tunes on the radio, and the Dallas skyline was in his rearview mirror.

He was headed home.

With a lot of luck, he'd get there in time for Sunday dinner.

After a few hours on the road, he stopped for hot coffee and called his brother. They still needed to talk about the holidays.

"Hey, Ford, got a couple of minutes to talk to your favorite brother?"

"Yeah, I just dropped Toby off for school. I've got some time to spare." He paused. "Where are you? That's not office sounds in the background."

He chuckled and scanned the landscape in front of him. "I'm almost into New Mexico."

"What are you talking about? You're usually in the office this time of day."

He tightened his hands on the steering wheel. "Not today." No way was he going to tell him exactly what was going on. It would ruin his surprise. "Just taking a little day trip."

"Good, you work too hard; hopefully, there's a special lady involved. Did Renee come to town?"

"No." Hank didn't respond to the rest of that comment and instead launched into his idea about the holidays. "Mom and Dad would be thrilled to have you and Toby from before Thanksgiving until after the New Year. What do you say?" He didn't bother to pretend to include the soon-to-be ex-wife in the plans; she was out of the picture permanently, even though Ford had yet to use the D-word.

"I might be able to arrange an extended vacation from work. I'll consider it."

Even though Ford couldn't see him, Hank was nodding. "Good. Well, I hope you'll give it some serious thought; it'd mean a lot to Mom and Dad, and Toby will have a blast, cutting down a tree and Santa's reindeer on the roof."

"All good times for sure."

Hank wanted his nephew to experience a good old-fashioned Montana holiday like they had as kids and who knows? Maybe Ford would decide it was a better place for them both.

"It's a good idea and I'll think it over. Can I let you know in a few days?" Ford's voice had a spark in it.

The unspoken question weighed heavy on Hank. "Yeah, of course, and bro, are you doing okay?"

"Some days are better than others, but we will be."

The sheen on his happiness dimmed a little when he heard his brother force out the sentence.

"Thanks for calling, Hank, and we'll talk soon."

"Sounds good, and Ford, if you want to talk, you know how to reach me." He ended the call and focused on the blacktop in front of him.

His next call was to Rob Adler.

When Rob answered and realized Hank was on the other end, he said, "It's been a while. How's life in Dallas?"

"That's why I'm calling. Is the offer to accept a desk in your office still available until you're ready to fully retire? Then I'd like to buy the practice." Hank held his breath as the seconds ticked by. If he had wasted a golden opportunity, he had only himself to blame.

With a chuckle, Rob said, "I think I can make room for you. When do you want to start?"

"I'll be in River Junction by Sunday. I'd like to come by Monday morning and check the office out and ask if you know of a decent place I can rent for a while."

If Rob was surprised, he didn't let on. "I've got just the place. Come by anytime on Monday and I'll let Corinne know you're coming in."

"That's fantastic. See you then, but do me a favor, and keep this just between us." Even if Rob had said no, he wasn't looking back. Dallas was his past and River Junction held his future.

State lines came and went. When he was within fifty miles of Wyoming, his eyes burned. It was time to take a much-needed break. The glare from the sun and now headlights were exhausting. He pulled into a motel for the night, pleased he was making good time and after a decent night's sleep, he'd be on the road again.

The next day, after an uneventful drive through Wyoming, signs for Montana welcomed him home. A few more hours and the next phase of his life would begin.

. . .

*H*ank stopped the SUV at the end of his parents' driveway. The windows were down and he took a few moments to inhale the sweet, fresh air of home. He could see Renee's pickup parked in the driveway and in a few minutes, she'd be in his arms. He eased forward, parked out of view of the house, and made the final few feet of his trip on foot. His hand rested on the doorknob, and he turned it quietly, savoring the anticipation of the surprise. Heart hammering in his chest, he touched his shirt pocket.

Strolling into the kitchen, he was disappointed they weren't sitting at the table, but voices from the dining room drifted his way. He toed off his boots and tiptoed to the doorway, hovering in the opening. Renee was looking away from the door, long waves of deep-red hair cascading down her back. Mom looked up and her mouth formed a small *O*. Dad's eyes grew wide, and Hank cleared his throat. "Do you have enough for one more?"

Renee turned in the chair, got up, and leaped into his arms, covering his face with kisses.

Her hands were on either side of his cheeks and confusion filled her eyes. "What are you doing here?"

"I heard Mom was making pot roast and those little potatoes I like, and I just can't get a decent homecooked meal in Dallas so here I am." He grinned and then pulled her to his chest, and for her ears alone, he asked, "Nice surprise?"

With a sob caught in her throat, she said, "The best. How long are you staying?"

His parents watched the reunion and he held out his hand for them to stay put. He had something to say and wanted them to hear it.

He eased her from his arms. "Renee, these last weeks have been torture, and I knew the minute I stepped on the plane that I was making a mistake. It took some time to get my head on straight and make a change."

Holding her left hand in his, he dropped to one knee and withdrew a diamond ring from his shirt pocket. "I hope you'll forgive me for taking so long to ask you a very important question, but I know where I want to be and who I want to be with."

Her free hand covered her trembling lips and she blinked tears from her eyes.

"Renee Mitchell, will you agree to marry me and live the rest of our lives in our hometown?"

She sank to her knees. "Hank, are you sure you want to leave Dallas?"

"Darlin', I already have. The condo's been listed; I resigned from the firm, and all that I wanted to keep is in the back of my SUV. So, marry me and make me the happiest man on earth."

She tenderly kissed his lips and wiped the dampness from his face. "I'll marry you on one condition."

"Name it, my love."

She tipped her head to the side. "I want us to get married during apple blossom time next spring."

He threw his head back and laughed, and then he kissed her again. "Under the apple blossoms in Montana it is."

EPILOGUE

Spring the Following Year

*R*enee smoothed her trembling hand over the ivory lace of her wedding dress. The last year had been a whirlwind filled with fun, laughter, and love—and today, Hank, the only man she had ever loved, would be waiting for her among the apple trees they had planted just one year ago. It was surreal thinking back to that day when she saw what she thought was her future squashed in the Montana dirt. What sprang from the fertile soil was so much more than she could have ever dreamed. Today, they would start their future together as husband and wife where this new romance had begun—sans the cattle.

She leaned into the mirror and checked her pale-pink lipstick. Satisfied with the long waves framing her face, her brown eyes were enhanced by the artfully applied makeup. It was sweet that her mom had insisted a professional hair and makeup artist come to the house for Renee's special day.

She crossed to the bedroom window and looked toward the main barn where the reception would be held.

She wanted to go out and triple-check that everything was set but she couldn't take the chance that Hank would see her roaming around in her bathrobe and Muck boots. She smiled when she thought that might send him running over the river and through the pastureland back to Stone's Throw Ranch. Instead, she closed her eyes and pictured the transformation. White gauzy fabric artfully draped from beams created a cozy, intimate feel; clear twinkle lights were everywhere, and vases of fresh-cut apple blossoms and pink roses adorned every table covered in pure white linens and pale-pink napkins. Soon, it would be filled with their friends and family celebrating their special day.

A soft tap on her door drew her attention and it eased open. She turned to see her parents holding hands, dressed in their wedding finery. Her dad was in his dark tuxedo with a pink apple blossom corsage in his lapel and her mom looked beautiful in a deep-green gown, the perfect shade, reminiscent of leaves on the apple trees.

"Sweetheart." Her mom stepped into the room and kissed her cheek. "The buggy is out front. Are you ready to find your groom?"

She pressed her hand to her midsection but that did nothing to quiet the butterflies dancing. Fanning her now warm cheeks, she said, "Why am I so nervous?"

"Today's the day you've been dreaming about since you were a little girl. Even when you were small and played wedding, you'd call that large teddy bear you used as the groom, Hank. Deep in your heart you always knew he was the only man for you."

She smiled and wrapped her arms around her mom. "He's an amazing guy and we're going to do great things with this farm, you wait and see. I promise we'll make you proud."

Her dad wrapped his arms around both of the women.

"We don't have to wait, honey—you already have, and Hank is darn lucky to be marrying you today."

Renee blinked away the tears. There was no way she had time to get her makeup fixed and she didn't want to keep her soon-to-be husband waiting one extra minute. After all, her mother was right; this had been a lifetime in the making.

"Thanks, Dad, for everything, your support, guidance, and for trusting me—well, us now—with the family's legacy."

He lovingly tapped her chin and smiled. "I was surprised when Hank wanted to become a lawyer-slash-farmer instead of a rancher but whatever makes you two happy is what makes me happy."

She threw her arms around her father and hugged him tight. "Thanks, Dad, you have no idea what that means to me."

*H*ank stood under the arbor in a clearing in the middle of the apple orchard, his hands clasped in front of him. The timing couldn't have been more perfect. For once Mother Nature had done exactly what she needed to do on time. The trees were in full blossom; the new trees that had been planted last year were growing, and the weather was mild; even the gentle drone from the bees at work added to the ambiance. It was the perfect day to marry the woman he loved.

He scanned the guests and it warmed his heart to see most of the residents of River Junction had come to share this day with him and Renee. His parents and Toby were in the front row. Ford was by his side as the best man. The wedding march swelled from the portable speakers. His breath caught.

Renee, with her mom on one side and her dad on the

other, began walking down the rose-petal-strewn path that led to him.

He swallowed the lump that formed in his throat; she was stunning.

The long lace gown softly swished around her ankles as she glided down the aisle. The glow on her face highlighted her soft-brown eyes which brimmed with love and happiness. It echoed what was in his heart.

It seemed to be taking forever for her to reach him. He walked up the aisle and met her halfway, his eyes locked on hers, never breaking their connection.

She stretched out her hand and he clasped it, fingers entwined as warmth spread over him.

He kissed her cheek and murmured, "Hi. I've been waiting for you." This was their day.

She laughed softly. "I hope I'm worth the wait."

He whispered, "I would have waited for this day for all eternity, but I'm glad I didn't have to."

He shook Dave's hand and kissed Sara's cheek. "Thank you." He felt the lump rise in his throat again. "I promise that Renee and I will live our best life right here." He glanced around. "We'll be good to the land and each other, always."

Dave clapped a hand on his shoulder and gave it a squeeze. "That is all Sara and I ever wanted, for Renee to be loved and love with all her heart."

"Oh, Daddy."

Hank withdrew a handkerchief from his jacket pocket, silently thanking his mom for insisting he put it there. He dabbed the dampness from his bride's cheeks. "Don't cry, Apple Queen."

She blinked away the drops that lingered on her bottom lashes. "Happy tears."

He bobbed his head in the direction of the minister. "Ready to start the rest of our lives?"

With a grin, she said, "More than ready."

They walked the last few steps hand in hand and when they stood in front of their friends and family, he looked at his mother. "Momma, get your hanky out. I'm about to marry the love of my life."

She held up a bit of cloth and nodded with a smile that filled her eyes with happiness.

He turned to Renee and took both of her hands in his.

The ceremony was a blur and they recited each vow in a clear voice.

There was no place he'd rather be than standing in the orchard with Renee, surrounded by nature, friends, and family.

The minister said the final blessing and then the words he had been waiting for his entire life. "Hank, you may kiss your bride."

He leaned in close and before his lips touched hers, he said, "I'll love you forever, my beautiful Montana bride."

Her eyes shone with happy tears. "And I will love you always plus one day, my husband." They sealed their future with a kiss.

If you loved **Second Chances in Montana** help other readers find this book: **Please leave a review now!**
Are you ready to read more about the Price family? Check out this sneak peek at Breathe, Book 1 in the Price Family set at Crescent Lake Winery series:

Her dream come true may be the end of his...

Her family's successful winery business in a small town in upstate New York should have gone to Tessa Price. She'd always dreamed of running the winery, but her brother, the prodigal son, has returned to claim the corner office.

Looking to prove to her family she's more than capable, she boldly strikes out on her own, purchasing Sand Creek Winery—a cash-strapped competitor—right out from under her family. She can forge her own destiny, using her marketing skills and big plans to bring new life to the small winery. But first she has a proposition for the sexy previous owner. And he's likely to hate it almost as much as he hates anyone with the last name of Price.

Kevin "Max" Maxwell would never have willingly sold his winery to anyone named Price. Family always comes first, and if paying for his sister's cancer treatment cost him his business, it was worth it. But when the new owner offers him a one-year contract to stay on as general manager, with a possible bonus, he's hit rock bottom but he really can't afford to turn it down. He can ignore the effect her deep brown eyes and heart-shaped face have on his senses for a year, can't he?

Relationships, like slowly ripening vineyards, take time. But Max has been keeping a secret from Tessa, one that could destroy their hopes for a future. Will a terrible accident force Tessa and Max to face how much they have to lose or tear apart their budding relationship forever? Sometimes a romance is like a fine wine. To be its best, it just needs time to breathe.
Keep reading for a sneak peek of
Breathe-
Price Family Romance Series
Featuring the amazing Tessa Price and the dashing Kevin, Max, Maxwell
Order Now

LUCINDA RACE

BREATHE

Price Family Romance Series

CHAPTER ONE

The moment Tessa opened the heavy wood and glass door, her eyes were drawn to the tall, open stairwell. Kevin Maxwell leaned against the steel and glass banister, watching her.

He greeted her with a flat smile. "Good morning, Ms. Price. Welcome to Sand Creek Winery."

The glass door closed behind her with a small whoosh. She squared her shoulders and walked into her winery. "Please call me Tessa."

He gave her a half nod. "Tessa."

"I'm glad you're here. I wanted to talk with you."

"I've been clearing out my"—he gave a slow shake of his head—"your office. I won't be long."

She ascended the stairwell. "Wait."

Kevin's cool blue eyes met hers. He was dressed casually in a crisp, cream-colored shirt, the cuffs rolled back, which highlighted strong hands and muscled forearms. He had high cheekbones, a long, thin nose, and was more handsome up close. She guessed he was around her age.

"I'd like to start our relationship on the right foot."

His eyes never left hers. Challenging her.

She had been right that he wasn't thrilled to see her. She had negotiated the purchase through a broker since she suspected he wouldn't sell to a Price, no matter how much money was involved. She'd made a fair offer and he'd accepted it.

She pointed to an open door. "After you."

He did a one-eighty and strode through the doorway.

The large room was dominated by a long maple conference table and several leather chairs. In front of her was a wall of windows that looked out over acre after acre of vines. Pride surged in her. It already felt like she belonged. Several boxes were strewn about, in various stages of being packed. Not seeing a desk, she set her black leather briefcase on the table and walked to the windows.

"Quite the view." Kevin had come to stand next to her. He was so close, she could feel the waves of indifference radiating off him.

Without looking at him, she said, "It looks completely different from this perspective. The virtual tour didn't do it justice."

"When I built this building, my intent was to be able to look out and witness nature as it nurtures the vines. Watching the vineyard throughout the seasons gives me hope for the future. There's nothing like it." He turned away as if he couldn't bear to look any longer.

"Impressive." She was reminded of the view in Don's office. It was strikingly similar. She turned from the window and gestured to the chairs at the table. "Please, can we talk?"

He dropped to a wooden stool, leaving the executive chair noticeably empty.

Unsure where to start, she said, "You can trust me with Sand Creek Winery." She empathized with how it must feel, forced to sell his business.

When she sat down, he gave her a curious look. "It was

either accept the blind offer or let the bank take it. I'll admit if I had known it was a Price, I might have reconsidered."

She cocked her head to the side and let that comment slide. "I have a proposition for you." She wanted to rephrase that, but it was already out there.

His eyebrow rose and his chin dropped a fraction of an inch. "I'm listening."

"I would like for you to stay on as the general manager."

She could have heard a pin drop.

"And why would I want to do that?"

She leaned forward and clasped her hands, resting them on the polished wooden surface. "You're a good wine-maker. I suspect a good marketing campaign can change sales. I happen to excel in sales and marketing."

"You think very highly of yourself."

She thought she saw a glimmer of humor in his crystal-blue eyes. "You know how to manage the field workers. You have a couple of excellent wines, but I want to hire an enologist to work with you, someone who is interested in growing this business."

Kevin leaned back in the chair and crossed his arms over his chest. "What's in it for me besides a paycheck?"

Available on all storefronts, *be sure to pick up your copy today.* **Order Breathe- Book 1**
Price Family Romance Series
Order Now

A FREE STORY FOR YOU

Have you enjoyed Second Chances in Montana? Not ready to stop reading yet? If you sign up for my newsletter at www.lucindarace.com/newsletter you will receive Blends, the love story of Sam and Sherry, right away as my thank-you gift for choosing to get my newsletter.

Can two hearts blend together for a life long love..

His mother's final illness waylaid Sam Price's college dreams, but he's content working in his family's vineyard in a small town in upstate New York. When he finds a woman with a flat tire on a vineyard road, he's stunned to discover it's the girl he'd had a crush on in high school. He'd never been confident enough to ask her out back then. He'd been a farm kid. Her daddy was the bank president. Way out of his league.

Sherry Jones is tired of her parents' ambitious plans for her life. She'll finish her college accounting degree like they want, but how can she tell them about her real love: working with growing things? Then a flat tire and a neglected garden offer her an unexpected opportunity, with the added bonus of a tall, gorgeous guy with eyes that set her senses tingling.

What does a guy with dirt under his nails and calluses on his hands have to offer a woman like Sherry? It will take courage for her to defy her parents and claim her own dreams. Sam and Sherry's lives took different paths, but a winding vineyard road has brought them back together. Are they willing to take a chance to create the perfect blend for a lifelong love?

Blends is only available by signing up for my newsletter – sign up for it here at www.lucindarace.com/newsletter

LUCINDA RACE

BLENDS

a crescent lake winery novella

SNEAK PEEK

Chapter One

Early 1980's... Sherry Jones kicked the gravel road with the toe of her bright-pink sandal. Pebbles flew across the road to the scrubby grass on the other side. A flat tire and she was in the middle of nothing but grapevines. She turned three hundred and sixty degrees. As far as the eye could see, vines.

Why did it have to be so damn hot today? It was spring, not mid-July or August. A trickle of sweat ran down her back. Whether she went right or left, it was going to be a long, hot walk. She knew how far the gas station was from the direction she had come from, so it was time to go the opposite way. She couldn't remember ever being in this part of Crescent Lake before. Surely she'd find a house or a gas station that was closer down this road, and hopefully someone would be around so she could use the phone.

She jammed her keys in her distressed short-shorts pocket and walked at a steady pace. She hadn't gone more than a quarter of a mile when a blister began to form between her big toe and the thong. In the distance, she could hear the faint rumble of thunder, or was that a truck?

If it was a storm, could her spring break get any worse? Last week, she broke up with Brad the cheater, her boyfriend of all of three months, and now she had to deal with a flat on her new used car, and a blister. She kicked off her sandals and walked in the sparse grass on the side of the road. There was a break in the never-ending field: another dirt road. The rumbling grew closer. A pickup truck slowed and came to a halt.

Her day just got worse. Arrogant and obnoxious, Sam Price stopped and leaned out the driver's window. "Well, look at you."

He flashed her a wide smile, his teeth even brighter against his tanned skin. She guessed it was from working outside all day. She hated to ask, but getting help was better than walking for miles, and it wasn't like he was the worst guy in the world. Just, they weren't friends.

"Hi, Sam." She shaded her eyes with her hand. "Any chance you know how to change a tire?"

"Sherry Jones, of all people to find wandering in my vineyard; of course I do. You don't drive around in trucks all day without knowing how to do simple repairs." His smile was broad, and his tone was slightly cocky.

She put a hand on her hip and glared at him. "Well, not everyone drives around in trucks all day." She wanted to snap at him but if she did, there'd be no way he'd help change her tire.

"Touché." He shrugged. "I'm gonna take off. See ya around." He looked toward the road in front of him. With a wave of his hand, he dropped the truck into gear and eased forward.

She groaned. "Sam. Wait."

He turned to her. His lips twitched as the smile grew wide.

"I'm sorry. Is there any chance you have time to change my tire?" She jerked her thumb over her shoulder. "My car is back that way and the passenger side is flat as a pancake."

He propped his arm in the open window and pointed to the seat. "Hop in."

She tossed the offending thong in the truck and climbed inside. "Thanks. I appreciate you taking the time to help."

He gave her a sidelong look. "Why are you limping?"

"Blister. My sandals aren't made for walking any distance."

"Just for looks?"

Was that his way of paying her a compliment or was he being a smart aleck? "Something like that."

He threw the truck in reverse with a slight jerk and did a three-point turn to go back in the direction she had come from. She wasn't sure what to say to make small talk. They bumped over the dirt road without talking. He whistled off-key, and she stared out the windshield.

"Thanks again for helping. I'm sure you're busy."

"I've got time." He pointed to a car off to the side of the road. "Is that you?"

She nodded.

"Glad to see you pulled off the road."

Annoyance bubbled up. "Do you think I'd just leave it so no one could get around?"

He held up a hand. "It's a dirt road. Not many people come this way." He looked at her. "What are you doing out here?"

"Just driving around." The last thing she was going to tell him was the real reason she was driving through endless miles of grapevines. She was hiding from the world.

He pulled off and parked. "Pop the trunk so we can get the jack and spare."

He walked next to her. She couldn't help but notice he had grown taller since graduation but he still had those molten brown eyes, long eyelashes, and bleached-blond hair. Even though he had a hat and sunglasses on, she remembered them and him. He was easy on the eyes, and all the girls had thought so in high school.

She unlocked the trunk and the lid sprang open. He lifted up the tire well. It was empty. She felt the color drain from her face. Now what? No spare and she was stuck.

"Sherry, what are you doing driving around without a spare tire?"

She threw up her hands. "How should I know? I just bought this car when I got home for spring break. Don't they always have them?"

He flicked the trunk closed and leaned against it. He pushed his ballcap back and propped his sunglasses on the brim. His deep-brown eyes were fixed on her.

"Did you check the trunk when you took it for a test drive?"

Crossing her arms over her chest, she said, "No." She tilted her chin up.

"You can't assume when you're buying a used car." He kicked some stones with his work boot, causing little puffs of dust to float in the air. He looked down the road as if weighing his options. "Get your stuff and I'll drive you home. But I need to stop at my house first. You can use the phone to call a tow truck."

"I don't want to put you out. I'll call my mom and she can pick me up."

He seemed to consider what he wanted to say next and gave her a sidelong look. "I'll drive you into town. I need to go to the hardware store anyway." He walked around to the driver's door and opened it. "But the tow truck can be on its way out here and you could get your car back tomorrow. Leave the keys under the mat and we can get going."

She didn't move. "Are you sure the car is safe with the keys in it?" She pursed her lips. She had been saving for the last three years to buy her first car and she didn't want to have it stolen. Her hard work would have been for nothing if that happened. Besides, in two short months, she would need it to drive to her first full-time job.

"Out here, we'd leave our keys in the ignition with a flat. No one would bother it. Your car is safe."

She looked from Sam to her car. It wasn't that she didn't want to believe him but— "I'm not sure."

He extended his hand but it never contacted hers. In spite of that lack of touch, the racing sensation down her arm felt like he had. His voice softened. "Trust me. If someone steals your wheels, I'll replace it."

"Well, that wouldn't be necessary." She looked at him. It felt like it was the first time she was seeing Sam. It was a cliché, but if eyes were the window to the soul, this brash guy had a gentle side. "Alright." She took her bookbag and rolled up the windows and then placed the keys underneath and in the center of the rubber floor mat.

***

Sam waited for her before he walked back to his truck. "I have to swing by the house before we head into town. I need to get my list for the hardware store. Now, when we get to my place, don't worry about the dogs. They're big and bark a lot but they're harmless."

When he had seen Sherry walking barefoot down the dirt road, her shoulders slumped, he had to stop and help. She was the one girl he had wanted to date in high school but had never asked. She was out of his league. Her mom was a high school English teacher and her dad was the president of a bank in Syracuse. His family worked the land. Not that he was ashamed that his fingernails had dirt under them and there were calluses on the palms of his hands. They had a great life and he wouldn't trade it for anything, but she was out of his dating pool.

"When we get to the house, I'll get you something to

put on your blister. You don't want to have it pop and get infected."

"Sam, you don't need to fuss over me." Her long blond ponytail swung from side to side. She looked like she was barely sixteen.

"How's college?"

"Two more months and then I have to start working full time."

He nodded as they drove. "Any ideas?"

"Office job. I'll have a degree in accounting, but it is so boring." She rolled her eyes.

With a chuckle, he asked, "Then why are you studying it?" He gave her a side-glance.

"My parents think it's a sound career choice. I might take the CPA exam."

"What's that?" He couldn't imagine not doing what he wanted to every day. It was like he had grape juice in his veins instead of blood. He loved the winemaking business. The ups and downs of a growing season, it was the ultimate thrill ride. This was something he wanted to do until he took his last breath.

"Certified public accountant." She released a heavy sigh. "I can become a controller for a company or something like that."

"I take it that's not for you." He saw the look of resignation on her face.

"I'll make a decent living, but doesn't it sound dull to go to an office every day for the next forty-plus years?"

Now he was curious. "What would you do if you could?"

She looked out the side window and waved her hand, trying to dismiss the question. "You'll laugh."

"Come on. Try me." Now he had to know. "If you tell me, I'll share a secret with you."

She gave him a curious look. He could tell she was trying to decide if she should or not.

"Landscape horticulturist."

It came out almost as a whisper.

She liked plants. He grinned. They had something in common after all. "Then why aren't you studying horticulture? Growing anything is gratifying." He pointed out the window to the passing landscape. "Look around you." The vines gave way to the long driveway leading to his parents' house. His mom always had beautiful flower gardens, but since she had passed away, they had become neglected.

Stately maple trees lined part of the drive as they grew closer to the house. "Don't look too close at the flower beds; they've been neglected the last couple of years."

Sherry's eyes were glued to them. Her eyes were bright as she saw the terraced gardens to the left of the road.

"Mom has, had, her vegetables there. She always had a huge garden and preserved a lot of what she grew. She also gave bushels of vegetables to the field workers each season." He smiled, remembering the baskets he'd have to lug down to the warehouses each afternoon after she harvested. Well, that was before he got involved with working in the fields to learn about the cultivation of grapes from Dad.

"Your mom doesn't garden anymore?"

"I guess you didn't hear." His hand tightened on the steering wheel and he swallowed the lump in his throat. "She died. Cancer." It still burned and probably always would.

She touched his arm with a featherlike gesture. "I'm sorry. I didn't know."

"It's just me and Dad now." He stopped the truck and looked at her. She curled her fingers into the palm of her hand. Silence filled the cab for the few moments they sat there. He could still feel the warmth of her touch.

He cleared his throat and mumbled, "Thanks." He pushed open the door. "Come on in."

She followed him to the back door. Two large German shepherds came racing around the corner at full speed. The scream died in her throat. They jumped against her and pushed her back. She stumbled. Sam put his arm out to catch her, but she still landed on her butt. They continued to bark. She cringed.

"Doc. Moe. Sit." Sam snapped his fingers. The barking ceased.

She was surprised to see the dogs' butts on the ground, and then they lay down, their heads resting on their paws. Sam extended his hand and pulled her to her feet.

"They won't hurt you."

In a few flicks, she brushed off her backside and straightened her top.

She glanced at them, suspicious. "Their teeth don't look harmless."

"They love people." He knelt on the ground and spoke quietly. Their ears twitched. "This is Sherry and she's my friend. Be nice."

She wasn't sure which dog was which, but first one's tail began to thump on the ground and then the other.

He looked up at her. "Do you want to pet them?"

She wasn't a dog person. Her parents had an old cat who spent her days and nights snoozing. Sherry was cautious but knelt on the ground in front of the dogs, feeling confident because of the way Sam looked at her. He had an intensity about him. Her pulse quickened and her eyes locked on his. "Okay," she breathed. But what she had just agreed to was anyone's guess.

Blends is only available by signing up for my newsletter – sign up for it here at www.lucindarace.com/newsletter

LOVE TO READ?

Cowboys of River Junction

Second Chances in Montana
Twenty years later Renee and Hank are back where they fell in love but reality is like a spring frost and is a long-distance relationship their only option for their second chance?

Stars Over Montana
The cowboy broke her heart but he never stopped loving her. Now she's back ready to run her grandfather's ranch...

Hiding in Montana
Can love flourish while danger lurks in the shadow?

Moonlight Over Montana
Will a single mom find love with the handsome cowboy who saved her and her daughter from danger?

The Sandy Bay Series
Sundaes on Sunday
A widowed school teacher and the airline pilot whose little girl is

determined to bring her daddy and the lady from the ice cream shop together for a second chance at love.

Last Man Standing/Always a Bridesmaid
<u>Barrett</u>
Has the last man standing finally met his match?

<u>Marie</u>
Career focused city girl discovers small town charm can lead to love.

Price Family Series
<u>Breathe</u>
Her dream come true may be the end of his...

Crush
The first time they met was fleeting, the second time restarted her heart.

<u>Blush</u>
He's always loved her, but he left. Now he's back...the question, does she still love him?

<u>Vintage</u>
He's an unexpected distraction, she gets his engine running...

<u>Bouquet</u>
Sweet second chances for a widow and the handsome billionaire...

Holiday Romance
<u>The Sugar Plum Inn</u>
The chef and the restaurant critic are about to come face to face.

Last Chance Beach
<u>Shamrocks are a Girl's Best Friend</u>
Will a bit of Irish luck and a matchmaking uncle give Kelly and Tric a chance to find love?

A Dickens Holiday Romance
<u>Holiday Heart Wishes</u>
Heartfelt wishes and holiday kisses...

Holly Berries and Hockey Pucks
Hockey, holidays, and a slap shot to the heart.

Christmas in July
She's the hometown girl with the hometown advantage. Right?

A Secret Santa Christmas
Christmas isn't Holly's thing, but will a family secret help her find the true meaning of Christmas?

It's Just Coffee Series 2020
The Matchmaker and The Marine
She vowed never to love again. His career in the Marines crushed his ability to love. Can undeniable chemistry and a leap of faith overcome their past?

The MacLellan Sisters Trilogy
Old and New
An enchanted heirloom wedding dress and a letter change three sisters lives forever as they fulfill their grandmothers last request try on the dress.
Borrowed
He's just a borrowed boyfriend. He might also be her true love.
Blue
Will an enchanted wedding dress work its magic one more time?

McKenna Family Series

Lost and Found
Love never ends... A widow who talks to her late husband and her handsome single neighbor who has secretly loved her for years.
The Journey Home
Where do you go to heal your heart? You make the journey home...
The Last First Kiss

When life handed Kate lemons, she baked.
<u>Ready to Soar</u>
Kate will fight for love, won't she?
<u>Love in the Looking Glass</u>
Will Ellie's first love be her last or will she become a ghost like her father?
<u>Magic in the Rain</u>
Dani's plan of hiding in plain sight may not have been the best idea.

Cozy Mystery Books

A Bookstore Cozy Mystery Series 2023
Welcome to Pembroke Cove, where witches and murders are multiplying...
<u>Books & Bribes</u>
It was an ordinary day until the book of Practical Magic conked Lily on the head causing her to see stars. And then she discovered her cat, Milo, could talk.

Catnap & Crimes
A witch, a snarky familiar and murder…

Tea & Trouble
When reading tea leaves turns to murder can Lily solve this latest case?

Scares & Dares
What does a haunted house and murder have in common? New witch Lily Michaels is determined to solve the case.

Holidays & Homicide
Even a fun event like the annual Glow & Glide can lose its charm when a body is discovered on the ice.

Leprechauns & Larceny

A leprechaun, a wedding, and pirate treasure, Oh My!

Magicians & Murder
When four magicians roll into town for a show more than
fun is on one person's mind.

Artifacts & Amulets Summer 2024
Milo has been keeping secrets, which can be deadly.

Cranberries & Criminals November 2024

SOCIAL MEDIA

Follow Me on Social Media

Like my Facebook page
Join Lucinda's Heart Racer's Reader Group on Facebook
Twitter @lucindarace
Instagram @lucindraceauthor
BookBub
Goodreads
Pinterest

ABOUT THE AUTHOR

Award-winning and best-selling author Lucinda Race is a lifelong fan of reading. As a young girl, she spent hours reading novels and getting lost in the fun and hope they represent. While her friends dreamed of becoming doctors and engineers, her dreams were to become a writer—a novelist.

As life twisted and turned, she found herself writing nonfiction but longed to turn to her true passion. After developing the storyline for A McKenna Family Romance, it was time to start living her dream. Her fingers practically fly over computer keys as she weaves stories of mystery and romance.

Lucinda lives with her two little dogs, a miniature long hair dachshund and a shih tzu mix rescue, in the rolling hills of western Massachusetts. When she's not at her day job, she's immersed in her fictional worlds. And if she's not writing romance or cozy mystery novels, she's reading everything she can get her hands on.